D1525455

Murder During the Antique Auction

A Mallory Beck Cozy Culinary Caper (Book 6)

Denise Jaden

Denise Jaden Books

No part of these books may be reproduced in any form or by any electronic or mechanical means without written permission from the author, except for the use of brief quotations in book reviews.

Thank you for respecting this author's work.

This is a work of fiction. Similarities to real people, places, or events are entirely coincidental.

MURDER DURING THE ANTIQUE AUCTION (A MALLORY BECK COZY CULINARY CAPER – BOOK 6)

First Edition. July, 2021.

Copyright © 2021 Denise Jaden

Written by Denise Jaden

All rights reserved.

Join my mystery readers' newsletter today!

SIGN UP NOW, AND you'll get access to a special mystery as well as bonus epilogues to accompany this series—an exclusive bonus for newsletter subscribers.

In addition, you'll be the first to hear about new releases and sales, and receive special excerpts and behind-the-scenes bonuses.

Visit the link below to sign up and receive your first bonus epilogue:

https://www.subscribepage.com/mysterysignup

Murder During the Antique Auction

A MALLORY BECK COZY Culinary Caper (Book 6)

Some people will kill for the perfect antique. The question is... who did?

When Mallory and Amber try their hand at catering their first event—an antique auction held on New Year's Eve—they have high hopes for helping the locals ring in the New Year with culinary decadence. But when a highly anticipated collector fails to show up and bid on a rare grandfather clock, the collector's daughter and the antique dealer are sure something is wrong.

Has the collector gone missing? Or was someone willing to kill him to get their hands on the prized antique?

Chapter One

NOTHING SAID BLACK TIE like eight dozen chocolate cappuccino cupcakes that were dressed up in fondant tuxedos.

Amber had spent countless hours molding decorations for the sweets and carving black olive accents for the savory appetizers we had prepared for our first catering event. My sixteen-year-old best friend and business partner insisted we pick a theme for the event, and after much deliberation, I'd chosen black tie from her many, *many* suggestions. It suited an antique auction on New Year's Eve, and I hoped it would elevate the evening.

Chad, the antique dealer in town who was putting on tonight's auction, met us at the door to the community hall. Chad was a slim man in his seventies with a gray ponytail and an ever-present twinkle in his eyes.

"Can I help?" He held out his hands, but Amber and I were not about to ask a senior citizen to help us carry in our culinary treats. Besides, we only had one tray each for the moment. Once we scoped out the space, we'd go back for the rest.

"Not at all," I said. "Just point us in the right direction, and we won't bother you a bit."

"Pshh. Bother." He waved a hand. "You ladies are sure to be the hit of the evening."

I hoped he was right, although my brief introduction to antique aficionados had taught me that many serious collectors had their eyes on little else.

"I was thinking I'd have you set up next to the clock." Chad led the way across the community hall.

A dozen or so people were busy setting up everything from doilies and old doll dresses to table and chair sets, all behind ropes in an arc around the perimeter of the room. The center of the room held about twenty rows of chairs, I guessed for the bidders. Chad led us to an empty table next to a roped-off ornately carved reddish-brown grandfather clock.

"It's my crowning triumph, and I'm sure every attendee will make their way by it multiple times this evening." He arrived at the empty table and turned toward us, looking at the two platters in our hands. "Is this table suitable?"

I suspected what he was really asking was if we had more in the car. I chuckled under my breath because boy, oh boy did we have more. "Actually, if there are any more tables around, we might grab a second one."

Chad's twinkle erupted into a full-blown spark. "You bet!" He rushed off. I hoped he knew we weren't expecting him to do the heavy lifting.

Amber placed her tray on the table. "We should probably get the bin with the tablecloths first, right?"

But she didn't wait for an answer and strode toward the door. She'd had an all-business attitude all day. I wanted to tell her to relax, but at the same time, I was nervous, too, and I wanted us to both do our best.

"For sure." I turned to follow her, but caught sight of Chad in the back corner of the large community hall trying to drag a fold-up table out of a storage room. "I'll be right behind you."

I rushed toward Chad, being careful to dodge all of the tables along the way. I glanced at silver candelabras and china teacups, wondering what kinds of prices each would garner. One lady worked her way around the room, carefully placing numbered bid cards in front of each item.

"Here, let me take that," I said to Chad when I was still several feet away.

Gratefulness crossed his face. "Why don't you just grab that other end, dear."

When I picked up the one end, I realized the table was actually lighter than it looked but awkward for one person.

By the time we had it set up, Amber had returned with our Rubbermaid bin of tablecloths and décor and another platter of cupcakes stacked on top.

"It's snowing again," she said. Her hair and the Rubbermaid bin were dotted with snowflakes. The local weatherman had been predicting an unseasonably cold winter, but lately, it had felt more like the blizzardy winters I'd endured in Pennsylvania. "I hope it doesn't affect your turnout."

"Oh, it won't." Chad sounded self-assured. "Antique collectors are not put off by much, and with this baby here tonight..." He motioned to the grandfather clock. "We're sure to draw a crowd all the way from New York."

I raised an unbelieving eyebrow, but I decided not to challenge Chad on this. Whether or not he was simply a positive thinker, I didn't know, but I was ignorant enough about the antique business that I wasn't about to challenge him on it.

Chad reached into the front of his tweed suit jacket and pulled out an envelope. "Can I give you your payment now?"

"Oh. Um. Are you sure you don't want to wait and see how we do?" I wasn't used to getting paid for delivering culinary treats. Even though I had spent a good amount of my own money on the ingredients for tonight, I would have been perfectly willing to eat the expenses, so to speak, so we could get our feet wet in this new catering venture of ours.

But Chad laughed at my question. "After those little drops of heaven you brought me at the shop a couple of weeks ago, I have no doubt everyone here tonight will be simply blown away."

While investigating a recent case, we'd delivered a container full of caramel rum tartlets to Chad at his antique shop.

It was how we'd talked some information out of him about a suspect, but also how we'd gotten the gig for tonight.

I fought my blush and accepted the envelope from him. "Well, then at least let me start you off with a cupcake."

I lifted the lid from the cupcake container Amber had just brought in, and Chad happily accepted an offering from the tray.

"Tuxedos!" he said. "I love it."

"We thought we'd do a black tie theme for tonight's event." Amber's words sounded like we did this all the time and this was simply one of our many themed events. I knew her well enough to hear the glow of pride behind her words.

"They're almost too pretty to eat." Despite his words, Chad took a large bite and then closed his eyes at the taste of coffee and chocolate. "I said *almost*."

Amber headed back for the car. "You'll have to come back once we're all set up. Chocolate cappuccino is only the beginning."

Chad's eyes widened in excitement, but I chuckled to try and quell his anticipation. I was pretty sure our treats would be well received tonight, but at the same time, I wanted to make sure to under-promise and over-deliver.

By the time Amber and I had set up a dozen varieties of sweet treats and savory items like triangles of brie with Dijon and black olives on Ritz to balance them out, the antique collectors had begun to arrive.

I recognized a few people, like Marv and Donna Mayberry and even our pastor from the Honeysuckle Grove Community Church. I wondered if they were serious collectors or simply here for something to do on New Year's Eve.

Chad had been correct, and there seemed to be a lot of out-of-towners I didn't recognize as well. He brought an unfamiliar stocky man in a navy suit our way to introduce us. "Mallory, Amber, this is my auctioneer, Roland Conway."

I reached out a hand to shake his, but Roland had his wide eyes on our refreshments and his hand already outstretched for a tangerine vanilla tea cake.

"You've outdone yourself this time, Chad." Roland looked at us almost as an afterthought. I had expected his words to come out fast and jumbled, being an auctioneer, but he spoke in an even, mid-pitch tone.

"These ladies just happened into my shop a couple of weeks ago with a few of their treats, and I knew right then that I had to somehow make our little auction attractive enough for them to attend." Chad winked at me in a way that might have made me feel disregarded by the other man, Roland, but from Chad, it was nothing but genuine.

Not that Amber and I had much to do with the bigger agenda tonight. We planned to keep the patrons happy as they strolled to view the wares, hopefully putting them in a more bid-friendly mood.

"No sign of Winston Blakely yet?" Roland scanned the room. Since I wasn't familiar with the name, I had to assume the question was directed toward Chad.

"Ah, you know Blakely." Chad sighed. "He's only coming for the one item, so he won't waste his time getting here early."

Chad and Roland took a long beat to survey the ornately carved grandfather clock, roped off beside our tables. Since the crowd for tonight had started arriving, a uniformed security guard had also been placed on the far side of the high-priced antique item. He regularly put his hands out to approaching guests, as if warning them not to get too close. I had yet to see anyone try, so it seemed like overkill.

"We're still starting the bidding at fifteen thousand?" Roland asked.

My eyes widened. I knew antiques were valuable, but fifteen thousand dollars for a starting bid? That seemed outrageous.

Chad scanned the room. "Yes. I don't see many here that will actually bid on it, but the bank insisted they needed that price at a minimum."

"The bank?" I asked.

Chad nodded. "This clock is from a foreclosure. Mayhew Bank delivered it this morning."

My stomach hollowed at his words. A year ago, my husband, Cooper, had died in a fire in that very building. The bank had been completely restored since then, but the mention of it brought me back as though it had happened yesterday.

"A foreclosure?" Amber asked. "Like someone got kicked out of their mansion and lost all their expensive possessions?"

When she went on with more questions, I could tell she was only trying to deflect the conversation from me. I kept a pasted-on smile in place, but she knew me well enough that she could probably tell I was struggling to catch my breath.

"It's from an estate," Chad explained. "A local man had all sorts of expensive antiques from all over the world, but it turned out that he had spent money he didn't really have. After he passed, his son, Ted, had to let the bank take most of it away to cover many years of back taxes." Chad pointed across the room to a bald man in jeans and a black T-shirt that stretched tight over muscular arms. "That's Ted there. I'll bet he came to see who walks off with his dad's clock."

The man looked more like a nightclub bouncer than a man concerned with antiques, but perhaps the clock had a personal significance for him. The clock was a bit gaudy for my taste, with porcelain accents on each corner and every inch covered with detailed carving, but I still felt bad for the man who must have been grieving his father and yet had to deal with the loss of all of his possessions from a bank.

I looked around the large room again, which had filled considerably. The serious collectors were obvious. They studied items from different angles, bending down or leaning across ropes to get a better look. A couple of them even had magnifying glasses out, and I saw one man investigating what looked like a cake platter made from Vaseline glass. I'd learned about the uranium-infused glass during our last case, and I wondered what kind of price the platter would garner.

"Uncle Ben and Aunt Bertie are here," Amber said. She didn't make any move to go and say hello, and Ben and Bertie didn't look terribly approachable, keeping their heads down and striding for some seats near the back section of chairs in the middle.

"Just awful what happened at their place." Chad shook his head.

Word had finally gotten around town about the fatal tiger attack that had happened on their property a couple of weeks ago. Ben held a bid card on his lap, as Amber's aunt and uncle were big collectors of antiques, but it looked as though they planned to get in and get out with zero chitchat tonight.

I didn't recognize any of the other serious collectors from Honeysuckle Grove. "This Winston Blakely, is he local?" I asked, recalling the name of the man they expected to walk away with the grandfather clock tonight.

"I'd better go and get my notes ready." Roland excused himself and headed for the podium on the stage, which left Chad to answer my question.

"Winston Blakely moved to Honeysuckle Grove in the summer to retire near his daughter. At least that's the story he gave, but word has it, he still keeps a business office in a cabin behind his mansion, where he spends most of his time."

"Does he deal in antiques?" I asked, surveying the expensive clock once again.

Chad chuckled. "Oh, no. That's just a hobby. Mr. Blakely owns Juniper Mills."

"The whole town?" I asked.

Chad shrugged. "Might as well. He owns the outlet mall there."

I'd been shopping at Juniper Mills a couple of times. It was worth the hour-and-a-half drive for the two hundred stores it boasted.

Chad raised his eyebrows. "Word has it that he owns other properties around the area, too, although he's pretty secretive as to which ones."

This made me think again about the property I'd found under Cooper's name on the Comptroller website. Cooper's bigwig literary agent in New York had suggested I could just head down to the local title deeds office to find out more about the property and the ownership. I'd never bothered, as I figured it was probably just an error, but I wondered if a curious person couldn't just do the same to find out more about this Winston Blakely's business acquisitions.

"So you don't think he's actually retired?" I asked.

"Who knows." Chad winked. "The way that man dresses and with his hard-as-nails personality, though? That makes me think he probably won't retire before the day he dies."

"And you don't own these antiques?" I motioned to the room filled with old precious items, still trying to get a handle on exactly how this worked.

Chad shrugged. "A few are from my store, but generally, for our New Year's Eve auction, I serve as the auction house."

"Auction house?"

"Folks list their items with me during the two months prior, let me know if they want a reserve bid posted, and then I take fifteen percent off the top if they sell."

I wondered if that would be a good income for one night's work. If the grandfather clock indeed sold for fifteen thousand dollars, that alone would garner him over two thousand dollars.

"There are a few high-demand items that serious collectors would kill for here tonight, but none quite as precious as this beautiful clock." Chad reached out as though he might touch the clock over the rope, but then retracted his hand before the security guard could raise an eyebrow.

A flurry of attendees made their way to our corner of the room right then, so I slipped behind our tables to help Amber while Chad excused himself to greet others arriving. I wondered if any of them were this Winston Blakely he'd spoken of, but from a distance, none of the new arrivals looked particularly serious.

As I served cupcakes, I asked attendees if they'd come to bid on a specific piece. Most laughed nervously at my question and said they'd only come for the excitement, and they couldn't actually afford most of the items up for auction tonight.

Donna Mayberry, always one to stir up mystery or gossip, informed me, "I like to play these things by ear. Maybe I'll bid on something, maybe I won't." Her voice carried from my table, no doubt to try and entice those around her to wonder what kind of a big spender she might be, but no one paid her any real attention. Even her husband, Marv, seemed to tune her out from only a few feet away.

"Would you like to try one of our chocolate cappuccino tuxedo cupcakes?" I asked Marv.

This he found interesting. "What? Oh, yes, Mallory. Anything of yours, I'm game."

When Cooper and I first moved to Honeysuckle Grove, Marv and Donna had been one of the most welcoming couples at the church, inviting us over for dinners in the winter and barbecues in the summer. They always told me not to bring anything, but I couldn't help myself and usually spent the day preparing some sort of fun and tasty side dish. I'd learned since then that Marv was a bit of a workaholic, working remotely for an advertising firm in New York City, while Donna didn't seem to have enough to do with her time and ended up spending much of it gossiping about others in the small town.

"I'm surprised to see you two here," I said as I passed him a cupcake on a black-and-cream-colored napkin.

Marv chuckled. "Donna wouldn't miss it. Everybody who's anybody comes to this thing."

He wasn't wrong. As the time clicked closer to eight o'clock, the community hall filled to capacity. There were about a hundred chairs lined up in rows through the center of the hall, but that wasn't nearly enough to seat everyone who had shown up. It seemed the serious bidders knew those chairs were for them and helped themselves to seats when Roland set up his notes and tested the microphone at the podium.

Donna Mayberry helped herself to a seat and placed a bid card on her lap. Even from my distance away, I could see her number read 79 in big block letters.

Chad came over to help himself to another cupcake as Roland announced the start of the festivities, and the audience began to settle. Once most of the chairs in the center were filled, a couple of dozen people still milled around the outer arc of wares.

A woman who looked to be eight or nine months pregnant in a hunter-green jumper approached Chad. "Where's my dad? He's never late, and he's been talking nonstop about that clock since it was added to your roster."

Chad surveyed the room. "I'm afraid I haven't seen him yet, Sheila. You're right, it is rather unusual for him to arrive late. He's assured me he would be taking this clock home tonight as well."

I glanced again at the grandfather clock, wondering if this was Winston Blakey's daughter, and what that would mean for Chad if his biggest ticket item didn't garner any bidders.

The lady in her early twenties—Sheila—sighed loudly, looking as though either this inconvenience or her pregnancy were exhausting her. Maybe both. "Well, I guess I'd better get a bid card." She rubbed her lower back and headed for the table near the hall's entry where a couple sat, writing down information from bidders and then passing them paddle-shaped cards to bid with.

By the time Roland finished his welcoming words to the crowd, Sheila had taken a seat in the back row with a card on her lap that read 148.

It seemed there would be almost a hundred and fifty bidders this evening. I wondered if that was more or less than what Chad expected, but he had disappeared into the fray of onlookers, so I didn't have a chance to ask.

Roland started the bids with a jade beaded necklace, which he described as Qing jewelry with Chinese motifs. He spoke in an even and understandable voice until he started the bid off at a hundred dollars. Then he slipped seamlessly into the fast tongue of any auctioneer I'd ever heard on television.

"One twenty, one twenty, do I hear one thirty?" Donna Mayberry's card flashed up, and Roland added, "We have one thirty from the lady in blue."

Donna Mayberry had worn a royal-blue pantsuit that looked striking on her long frame. Something about her actually bidding on antiques surprised me—perhaps because I had been to her home, and everything in it seemed ultra-modern. When the bidding hit three hundred dollars, though, her other hand rested on her bidding card as though she was holding it down through the rest of this auction.

Roland glanced over at a woman seated near him on the stage with a laptop open to take notes. She shook her head at him, and then Roland confirmed the winning bid of three hundred and eighty dollars to bidder number twenty-nine into the microphone. The woman typed this in, and Roland moved onto the next item, an English bone china tea set.

The auction continued with item after item, and the evening seemed to run like a well-oiled machine. The Vaseline glass cake platter only had three bidders and ended on a measly forty-five dollars. I soon tired of standing behind my table, and I could sense others around the room who weren't in on the bidding action starting to fidget, so I helped myself to a tray of mixed goodies and a stack of napkins and told Amber I was going to take a walk around the room.

I kept to the outskirts, so as not to disturb the bidding action, and was surprised to see my friend from the church's children's ministry, Sasha Mills, in attendance. Sasha was in her fifties and, other than some gray wisps in her hair, looked identical to how she had when she'd been my seventh-grade teacher so many years ago. I sidled up beside her, and when she looked over my tray of delicacies, I directed her to a fudgy brownie bite I knew a chocolate lover like her would enjoy.

"You're catering?" she whispered.

I nodded and glanced back toward our tables where Amber was now slumped into a chair, scrolling on her phone. "Amber and I are trying it out to see if we should make it a regular thing."

"You know, I think it's wonderful that you've taken such an interest in Amber after her father's death. I'm sure she appreciates having someone to talk to. But do you think Amber's up for that kind of responsibility?" Sasha wasn't the first person in my life to mistake my time with Amber as something I was doing solely for her, and she wasn't the first person to dissuade me from putting all of my hope and trust into a sixteen-year-old. But most people didn't know Amber the way I did. The reason she was so easily bored was because her speedy brain activity needed to be constantly stimulated. Give her something to do, or even many things to do, and she was more than capable.

Give her nothing to do, such as at an antique auction where people were too busy bidding to eat, and she'd probably have her college essays written on her phone's note program by the intermission.

"I'm certain she is," I told Sasha. "I'm trying to decide if *I'm* up for the commitment."

Sasha smiled as though I was joking. She'd only really known Amber as a small child in her class years ago at the elementary school.

"You should come out with the lunch ladies this week," she suggested.

The lunch ladies weren't actual lunch ladies, but simply a group of ladies from town who ate lunch together once or twice a month. Sasha had invited me one time before, but when I dropped a hint about inviting Amber and had gotten a laugh and a "Can you imagine?" type of response, I'd ended up claiming busyness.

Getting to know some local ladies my own age would probably be good for me, I decided. "Sure. Just text me the time and place."

I was getting to know Sasha more and more since helping out with the kids at church. This would be a good opportunity to tell her more about Amber's special talents when I could speak at a normal volume, but for now, I moved on just as Roland announced an antique dining set—an item too big to bring up to the stage, but he motioned toward it just below him at the foot of the stage.

He talked about the refurbishing efforts of the owners and then said, "Bidding starts at thirteen hundred dollars."

I was glad to hear the value of the items increasing, and the bidders were certainly active, so Chad would be sure to make some money.

As I moved past the entryway toward the other side of onlookers, an unshaven young man swept in through the door in a blue plaid jacket and a cowboy hat.

The man headed straight for the pregnant lady, Sheila, in the back row, and while Roland's assistant marked down the sale of the dining set and he moved onto the next item, the young couple had a hushed but animated conversation.

People stared at them, and my knee-jerk reaction was to defuse the tension with food. I strode forward through the middle row of seats and whispered loudly for all to hear, "Could I offer anyone a little snack?"

Several bidders took me up on it, standing from their seats and helping themselves to napkins and then sweet treats. A cleared throat at the microphone made me look up at Roland's annoyed face.

Oops. It seemed I'd only compounded the problem.

I smiled an apologetic smile and then backed my way down the aisle while Roland announced the next item on the roster. As I passed Sheila and the man in the cowboy hat, I heard him whisper, "Are you kidding me? We can't afford that, Sheels! And what if your dad won't pay?"

Another cleared throat, and I couldn't tell whether Roland was glaring at me or at the arguing couple. I decided in an instant I'd at least get myself out of the line of his glare, and I disappeared back into the outskirts of the room.

Soon after that, Roland held an intermission. I hoped it was scheduled, and he wasn't simply doing it because he was annoyed with all the distractions. I skirted behind our tables to help Amber as a crowd quickly swarmed the area, ready for a mid-meeting pick-me-up.

By the time Roland announced the commencement of the auction, our tables were almost cleared of anything edible.

"Maybe we should have made more," Amber observed.

We still had our midnight truffles packed away for later, but she was right. I thought we'd prepared more than enough for tonight, but many patrons had helped themselves to three or even four different treats each, which we hadn't been anticipating.

As if her observation didn't make me feel bad enough, Donna Mayberry was lurking nearby and tsked, shaking her head at my table. "Too bad you don't have any of those tuxedo cupcakes left. Those were my favorite."

She'd had three.

I was lost in thought over the depleted baking, so it took me a minute to clue in when Roland motioned in our direction and announced over the microphone that he was resuming with the final auction of the evening. Every person's gaze moved to the grandfather clock beside us, and I felt awkward and embarrassed by the state of our scant and disorganized tables.

Roland announced the starting bid of fifteen thousand dollars, and thankfully, this brought the attention back to him. The lady making notes beside him got his attention and tapped her cell phone. A moment later, she appeared to be speaking into it, from right beside him on the stage.

"What's happening?" I whispered to Donna, as she had been to more of these types of events than me.

"Oh, that?" She motioned to the woman with the phone and Roland, who was at a silent standstill at his microphone. "Someone must be phoning in their bid."

"You can do that?" That seemed pretty big-time for such a small town. Then again, Chad seemed proficient at running these auctions and had clearly garnered a following.

Donna shrugged. "Sure. I don't know why anyone would want to. Isn't the excitement of it being here in person to compete for the items you want?"

With that, Donna took her cupcake back to her seat. She and Marv had bid on several items this evening, but had not won any of the auctions. Now it suddenly made sense why Donna seemed ambivalent about it. She truly was only here for the excitement. She didn't care if she actually went home with anything.

Roland cleared his throat and officially started the bidding at fifteen thousand dollars. He glanced beside him to the lady on the phone, who nodded in response.

"We have fifteen thousand dollars. Do I hear sixteen thousand? Sixteen thousand?" He moved seamlessly into his quick auctioneer tongue.

A man in wire-rimmed glasses on the far side of the room flashed his bid card, and then Donna flipped hers up. I grinned and leaned toward Amber. "Watch. I think Donna Mayberry is only bidding up the item for a little excitement."

The pregnant lady, Sheila, held up her card, and I remembered that her father was supposed to be here to bid on the grandfather clock. I glanced back to the woman on the stage with her phone to her ear, who gave another nod, and I wondered if that could be Sheila's father on the phone.

Was she bidding against her own father to try and win the item for him?

I nibbled my lip. I didn't know the woman. It was none of my business, and I was certain Roland would have a fit if I made my way back toward the seated bidders to interfere again.

Three other people from around the room joined in on the bidding, and the muscular man who had lost the clock to the bank watched from the back of the room with his arms crossed. The price went up and up. Soon it was nearing twenty-five thousand dollars. Donna dropped out of the race after two others in the room hesitated with their bid paddles. Worry lines etched Sheila's face, and she took longer and longer to raise her paddle. Roland's smooth speech was the only thing that remained quick and calm in the room.

"Twenty-five thousand, four hundred going once..." Roland stared at Sheila with raised eyebrows. This last bid had come through the phone. "Going twice..." Sheila sucked in her lips, bowed her head to her lap, and shook her head slowly back and forth. "Sold to our bidder on the phone for twenty-five thousand, four hundred dollars."

Roland quietly spoke with the lady beside him for a moment and then returned to the microphone to thank everyone for joining him for the auction. But the second the winner of the clock had been announced, a hubbub rose over the room. People started to move from their seats. Ted Callaghan, the muscular man who had just watched his dad's clock go to a new owner, turned and strode for the door.

I checked my watch, and it was eleven thirty. Thankfully, Amber and I had prepared special truffles for midnight, and Chad returned to our tables with one of his assistants, carrying a case of champagne.

"Where's Alex?" Amber asked. She'd asked me this once earlier as well, but I'd been able to change the subject, as our cupcake tower had been depleted.

I shrugged. "He was supposed to be here."

An old-time fiddle trio took the stage, and the lights around the community hall dimmed. Along the walls, white twinkle lights glimmered, giving the room a celebratory feel.

As someone entered, I looked to the door, hoping it was finally Alex arriving, but it was just the young guy in the cowboy hat again, along with an older man with thick gray sideburns.

"Still no Alex, huh?" Amber asked, reading my mind as usual.

I sighed. "I hope everything's okay with him."

"Why wouldn't it be?"

Our closest friend, Detective Alex Martinez, had been keeping his distance ever since our private little Christmas celebration with just the three of us at my house. I'd had my suspicions that he'd been shaken up about getting shot in the line of duty and just wasn't ready to admit it. I had been shaken up.

But for all I knew, I was just projecting my own issues onto him. So I said, "Oh, I'm sure he is. He's just been so busy lately." Before she could push further into this conversation, I changed the subject and pointed to where Mr. Cowboy Hat seemed to be arguing with his pregnant wife again. "What do you think that's all about? Do you think he heard she'd been bidding into the twenties of thousands for the grandfather clock?"

The young guy certainly didn't look as though he had that kind of cash to spare, and I'd mentioned to Amber the argument I'd overheard between them earlier.

Thankfully, Amber took my lead with the change of topic. "And who's the old guy? He looks like he could be the guy's dad."

The man with the gray sideburns lurked near the couple, his arms folded over his chest, certainly hearing every word of their argument, but he turned away as if pretending to watch the security officer and another man wrap the grandfather clock in a blanket, secure it to a furniture dolly, and prepare to move it.

I may not have noticed the resemblance if Amber hadn't picked up on it. But now that she'd mentioned it, I could see that the two men frowned in a similar way and even held their posture, now with hands on their hips, in a similar fashion. "I'll bet you're right."

The fiddle music started up, and Chad and the woman who had been taking the phone bids filled our mostly empty table with half-full champagne flutes. Amber and I arranged our midnight truffles on the other table.

"They don't waste any time in getting the winning antiques out of here, do they?" I asked Chad, motioning to where the two men wheeled the wrapped clock toward the door.

"Most people will pay out and take their items with them when they leave tonight, but because our prize offering was won by a phone bidder, we want to make sure to keep it safe at a secure storage facility until we can deliver it tomorrow."

"Was it the man you expected to win?" I glanced again at Sheila, arguing with Mr. Cowboy Hat. "Winston Blakely?"

Chad shook his head. "No, surprisingly, it was a man calling from Juniper Mills. One I've never met."

Juniper Mills, home to Winston Blakely's outlet mall. Interesting coincidence that someone from that same town had won the clock Mr. Blakely had wanted. Then again, after solving so many murder investigations, my mind was often in hyperdrive, looking for coincidences. It likely didn't mean anything.

"Huh. So Winston Blakely didn't bid at all?" I didn't know the man from Adam, but I could feel Sheila Blakely's stress over the subject.

"His daughter, Miss Blakely, was bidding on his behalf. To be honest, I'm surprised she gave up so quickly."

I wasn't sure I considered twenty-five thousand dollars "quickly," but I didn't argue. From across the room, I could see the worry lines on her face. She had apparently been right to bid on her father's behalf. He clearly had money, if he owned Juniper Mills. I wondered if she'd reluctantly given up on the bidding because of her concerned husband. Perhaps that was why they were still arguing.

Before Chad had a chance to tell me anything more, Roland Conway strode purposely our way and spoke without seeming to notice if he was interrupting anything. "I want to get out of here. Can I get my money now?"

Chad glanced toward the table near the door. "Have you gone over the bid list with Sara?"

I found it curious that Chad had so easily offered to pay me in advance, yet he double-checked that Roland had finished all of his duties before offering him payment. Considering Roland seemed to have worked for Chad many times before, I found this extra curious.

Roland scowled. "Of course."

Then again, Roland had a chip on his shoulder about something. I suppose a person like that might not have finished their assigned work sometime in the past.

"You're not staying until midnight?" I asked, holding out my tray of truffles toward him.

He ignored my offering and picked at some frays along the edge of his suit jacket. "The last place I want to be at midnight is hobnobbing with the richies." He said the words to me, I was pretty sure, but kept his eyes on Chad as though he expected a challenge.

Leave it to an auctioneer to have a chip on his shoulder about people with money. Ah, the irony.

Chad passed over an envelope, and Roland opened it in front of him and double-checked the amount before offering a curt nod, turning on his heel, and heading for the door.

"Not the friendliest guy, is he?" Amber asked from beside me.

Chad sighed. "He's the best auctioneer around here, so we put up with him. The poor guy has had several business deals go bad over the years and always seems to be climbing out of some sort of debt every time I see him."

So it made sense why he had a chip on his shoulder. It was probably good that he'd left before midnight, so he wouldn't ruin the fun for everyone else.

Before I had a chance to ask more about him, Mr. Cowboy Hat and his dad marched back out the door.

Sheila Blakely headed our way. "Something's wrong, Chad. My dad should have been here."

Chad nodded. "Yes, dear, I thought so, too, but you know we can't hold auction items. The bidding starts when the bidding starts." Chad said this in a sympathetic tone, but it sounded practiced, as though he'd given this same speech a thousand times.

"No, of course. I know." She fiddled with the hem of a maternity cardigan she'd thrown on over her jumper. "It's not the clock. It's just...well, I'm really worried. He's not answering his phone. Not even his cell phone."

Chad adopted a fatherly tone. "Oh, sweetheart, I'm sure he's fine. You know your father gets busy."

She shook her head. "But not too busy for *this*. He's been talking about that clock for months. He desperately wanted it before the baby was born. I wonder if I should drive out to his place and check on him."

I tilted my head in confusion over what owning a clock had to do with her unborn baby.

Chad glanced toward the door. "Have you been outside, Sheila? It's been snowing all evening, and I'm certain the road out to his place hasn't been plowed. Can Dylan take you?"

She shook her head. "He had to get home to bed. He gets up early."

I wondered if Dylan was Mr. Cowboy Hat. I, too, wouldn't want to see this pregnant lady venture into a rural area in the middle of a snowstorm. I couldn't help offering to help. "I have a friend in the police department," I said. "If you give me his address, I can see if they could send someone out to check on him."

Sheila's worried eyes darted quickly to me. "Would you? He lives up in Breckendale Ridge." Then she rattled off an address, and I jotted it onto the notepad from my purse.

In truth, I'd been looking for a reason to call Alex. Maybe I could talk to him at midnight on New Year's Eve, even if I couldn't have him here. At the same time, I did want to help this poor distraught woman.

"Absolutely," I told her. "Enjoy the party, and I'll come and find you when I hear anything."

Chapter Two

I STEPPED OUTSIDE THE main doors of the community hall where it was a little quieter and pulled out my phone.

Alex picked up on the second ring and sounded surprisingly wide awake. I guess I expected that, if he chose not to hang out with us at the auction tonight, he'd be at home in bed already. My next call would have been to the local police station to see if Detective Reinhart happened to be around. While I was much better friends with Alex, Detective Reinhart—Steve—had taken me out on a date and expressed interest more than once, so I was quite sure he'd help me out if I asked.

"What's up, Mal?" Alex said from the other end, as I was lost in thought and had yet to say hello.

"Oh, I'm just over at the antique auction..." I left a pause, wondering if he would insert an excuse of why he hadn't stopped by. He didn't. "There's a very pregnant lady here who's worried about her dad, a Mr. Winston Blakely? Apparently, he was supposed to be here to bid on a grandfather clock tonight and never turned up. She was going to head out to his house to check on him, but in her condition and with the roads the way they are tonight, I guess I hoped there might be an officer who wouldn't mind taking a trip out that way."

When I said it out loud, I realized I was probably asking too much. If the man had only been missing for this evening, it seemed a lot to ask the very small police force of Honeysuckle Grove to get on the case.

But Alex said, "Sure. I can do it. I was just about to head home anyway."

"You're still at the station?"

The snow had stopped for the moment, and the security guard and the man helping him were busy loading the grandfather clock into a cube van. It was already wrapped in moving blankets, and they proceeded to secure it with bungee cords to the side of the van. The cube van was filled with other boxes and a table and chair set I could see from my vantage point on the front steps, all packed tightly against each other with moving blankets between.

"Yeah, I guess I lost track of time. Sorry I didn't make it by tonight." As he said the words, I squashed down my pang of disappointment. Not only had he not come by the auction as he was supposed to, but if I hadn't called, he wouldn't have even picked up the phone to offer any kind of excuse. Still, deep down, I didn't believe this had been a purposeful oversight.

Part of me wanted to tell him that if he headed straight here, we could still ring in the New Year together. But the bigger part of me knew if he was willing to check on Sheila's father, that was probably the more important objective.

"Well, if you have so much work, it has to get done, right?"

"Right," was all Alex said in reply, which only fed my suspicions that he was keeping some of his personal trauma under wraps.

As the cube van pulled away, I saw Roland sitting in an old pickup truck behind where it had been. He appeared to be typing into his phone, but a second after the cube van left, he pulled onto the main road after it.

I opened my mouth to tell Alex about the crabby auctioneer and the whole exciting night, but he cut me off before I could speak. "Listen, Mal, I'm pretty tired. Give me the address, and I'll head over there right away. And if you want to give me

Sheila Blakely's number, I can call her directly, so you don't have to wait up."

I waved a casual hand, even though he wouldn't be able to see it. "Just call me and I can relay the message." Besides the fact that I didn't actually have Sheila Blakely's phone number, I now had the distinct impression Alex was trying to avoid me. I wanted to get through to him that if something was wrong, I, of anybody, would understand if he was shaken up.

But I couldn't exactly do that when he'd just told me he had to go if he wanted to help.

"Just call me back when you're done," I said again. "Amber and I have lots of packing up to do before we can go to bed anyway."

Sheila Blakely approached me as soon as I stepped back into the community center. "What did you find out? Should I head out there myself?" Her speech was fast and shaky.

I pushed my hands toward the floor. Whether from pregnancy hormones or true concern over her father, her worry had skyrocketed since I'd left the building only five minutes ago. "My friend Detective Martinez is going to drive out to check on your dad himself. I don't know how far it is from the police station, but he said he'd go straight there and then call me back."

Sheila let out a sigh of relief. "Okay, thank you very much."

I led her toward a chair. The ones in the center of the room had been cleared, and several people were now kicking up their heels and dancing, but a few chairs were still scattered around the perimeter of the room. "You should rest. It's really late for you, I'm sure, and if you wanted to just head home, I could call you when I hear from Detective Martinez?"

Sheila shook her head. "Oh, I couldn't. I'll wait here until he calls you to let you know Dad's okay."

I assured Sheila I would tell her the second I heard from Alex and then headed back to see how Amber was doing with the truffles.

"We're out," Amber said as soon as I walked up. She slid our empty truffle tray sideways into one of our Rubbermaid bins. "But I'm pretty sure everyone who wanted one got one. Pretty sure a lot of them got four or five." Her voice was tinged in false modesty. She'd made the truffles last night, all on her own.

"We'll know for next time, then, won't we?"

"Next time?" Amber stopped mid-wipe of the table to stare at me, her face bright like the sun had just come up again. "We're going to do the catering business?" Her voice was giddy.

I sighed. I was too tired to properly watch my words. It wasn't as though I *didn't* want to start a catering business with Amber. But I had to rein in her enthusiasm a little or she'd have me selling my house tomorrow to buy a food truck.

"We'll talk about it," I told her in my most level tone. "But I'm certainly open to trying it again if you are."

As I helped clean up, my comments were enough to get Amber prattling on about *A Catering Company Unlike Any Other.*

I took two trips to the car, hoping she'd calm down, but while I grew more and more tired, she seemed to buzz with extra energy. I had to admit, she had some good ideas. But when she got to the part about taking out a full-page spread in the local newspaper, I had to stop her.

"If we do this, we have to start small," I said, but then my phone buzzed and I had to cut off my words and grab for it.

Just as I answered, the fiddle trio stopped playing, and Chad took the stage to announce the countdown to midnight. "Ten, nine, eight..."

Well, I supposed I'd gotten what I wanted, I mused to myself. I got to spend the turn into the New Year with Alex, if only by telephone.

"Seven, six, five..."

"Hello?" I said into the phone, rushing toward the door to the parking lot. It was soon going to be much too loud in here to be able to hear a word of what he said. Sheila tracked my progress, and I had no doubt she would follow me outside.

"Mallory, it's me," Alex said. He didn't sound right.

"Three, two, one..." Chad's voice got louder as I reached for the door handle.

"I'm afraid I have some bad news. I found Winston Blakely, but he's not okay."

"What?"

I reached the outside as Chad announced, "Happy New Year!" There were several couples out in the snow ready to kiss at the stroke of midnight.

"What do you mean, not okay?"

Sure enough, Sheila Blakely followed me out, and she stared at me with wide, worried eyes.

"He's in his office, but he's not breathing. He hasn't been breathing in quite some time, Mallory." Alex took in a heavy breath. "Winston Blakely is dead."

Chapter Three

"WHAT? WHAT'S WRONG WITH my dad?" Sheila asked, a frantic contrast to the couples outside who were lost in each other's comforting embrace.

I shook my head. There were few things I could imagine worse than delivering this kind of horrific news to loved ones. I wished I could wait for Alex to come and give the news himself, but he had to wait for the medical examiner and ambulance. It was up to me to tell Sheila.

"The news isn't good, Ms. Blakely."

"It's Miss Blakely. But call me Sheila." She shook her head as she seemed to realize this distinction was not important at the moment. "What news? What's not good?"

"Detective Martinez found your dad in his office. He wasn't breathing, Miss... Sheila." I stroked her shoulder as her eyes erupted in tears and the truth of the matter came over her. "The detective thinks it was a problem with the generator he had running."

"Carbon monoxide poisoning?" she asked through her tears.

"We'll know more when the medical examiner arrives, but that's what Detective Martinez suspects, yes."

"I have to get out there to see him." She marched toward the parking lot, so grief-stricken she didn't seem to notice she hadn't brought her coat or purse. I wondered if she even had car keys with her.

"Sheila, listen. Where's your husband...?" I recalled her calling herself Miss Blakely and corrected my wording. "Or boyfriend, or whoever you were with? The snow is awful out here, and if your dad had the generator hooked up, the power must've gone out as well. It's not safe for you to go alone, not in your condition."

She shook her head. "Dylan had to leave. I'm sure he's already in bed, and I can't wait. Please understand. I have to go and see my dad!"

I did understand, all too well. If there'd been any chance at all of seeing my late husband, Cooper, at the place where he'd died with my own eyes, it likely would have helped the reality set in. But he'd died in a fire where I couldn't get anywhere near him, and instead, I'd woken up day after day for months, reliving the realization that he was truly gone.

"Listen, I do understand," I told her. "And if you have to go, I believe you, and that's fine. But I'm not about to let you go alone."

I took Sheila by the arm and guided her back inside, afraid if I left her outside to wait for me that she'd either freeze to death or start walking toward her dad's house.

We got to the catering table where I'd left my coat and purse, and I told Amber, "I'm going to accompany Miss Blakely out to her father's place." I looked at Amber with serious eyes, hoping she could read the severity of the situation.

She nodded slowly. "Should I come along?"

Sheila let out a loud cry into her hands. Amber was amazing at a lot of things, but sympathy wasn't usually her strong suit.

"Do you mind finishing tidying up?" I looked around the room. "I wonder if I could get the Mayberrys or Chad to drive you—"

My words were cut off when another frantic cry rose up among the fiddle music. This time it was Chad, and I immediately thought he must have heard about Mr. Blakely.

He had a phone to his ear as he said, "Nooooo!" so loud that the fiddle players stopped. "Where? How?"

He was near the door, so it was on our way out. I hadn't realized he had been close to Winston Blakely, but I could at least offer some comforting words on our way.

"Are you okay, Chad? You must have heard the news," I said as he hung up, his face wide-eyed and shocked.

He snapped his gaze to me. "How did you hear?"

"My detective friend, he called and—"

"A detective's already there? Oh, thank goodness! Did they find out who did it? Please! You have to tell me they caught the guy!"

I pulled back. Alex hadn't indicated any foul play in Winston Blakely's death. I opened my mouth, but had a sudden check in my spirit and changed tacks on a dime. "What are we talking about here?" I asked.

"My delivery guy's cube van." He shook his head, still looking stunned. "It was run off the road. The grandfather clock worth over twenty-five thousand dollars was stolen!"

I sucked in a breath.

None of this was a good way to start off the New Year.

Chapter Four

BY THE TIME I'D gotten the little information Chad knew out of him and calmed him down, Amber had completely cleaned up our corner of the community center. Granted, there was a lot less to do now that we weren't trying to keep any sweets and treats looking display-ready, and there was much less to carry back to my car.

"I'll just have to drop off my catering partner on our way," I told Sheila as I led the way to my white Prius, which was almost invisible with a foot of snow piled on top.

"No, I'll go along," Amber said—I wasn't sure if to Sheila or to me.

I grabbed my ice scraper and broom from the trunk and reached in to start up my car. "You get inside and try to stay warm," I instructed Sheila.

I held out my two items, and Amber helped herself to the scraper, which was probably better. I was a couple of inches taller and would have an easier time sweeping the snow off the roof.

"Your mom will want you home before it gets too late," I explained as we worked. The last thing I wanted was to get into more hot water with Helen Montrose, who already wasn't crazy about me spending so much time with her six-teen-year-old daughter.

"Um, *actually,* she wanted me out tonight."

By her emphasis, I didn't think she was lying. "Out of the house? Why would she want that?"

Amber shrugged, and I felt bad that this was the first time I was even asking about her home life today. Maybe her attitude today hadn't been all-business. Maybe it had been self-protective. After losing her dad six months ago, her mom had been fairly checked out emotionally, dealing with her grief. I tried to be the sounding board Amber needed whenever we got together, but tonight, I'd been so consumed with our catering venture, it hadn't occurred to me to ask.

"She actually said she wanted you out of the house?" I pressed her as we slid the Rubbermaid bins of our supplies into the trunk and then got into the car, with Amber in the back and Sheila in the passenger seat. One thing I was thankful about with my Prius was that it heated up quickly in the winter and cooled quickly in the summer.

"She said, 'You can stay at Mallory's tonight, right?'" Before I could ask if Amber could have gotten the inflection wrong, she added, "I guess I just assumed I could. Sorry I didn't ask." Amber used a sarcastic tone, but I could hear an underlying current of insecurity.

Helen Montrose's sudden plea for Amber to spend *more* time with me was strange. More than strange. I had a quick vision of Helen waiting until her two teenage kids were out for the evening and then swallowing a full bottle of sleeping pills—dealing with her pain the only way she knew how.

"Turn right at the light," Sheila told me. Her sobs had subsided some since I'd first broken the news about her father. Now, she seemed solely focused on getting to his house as quickly as possible.

I hesitated at the light. Amber's house was in the opposite direction. But if I turned to go there, when Amber knew she had full permission to spend the night at my place, she'd know something was wrong.

One tragedy at a time, I told myself. And then I turned right, toward Winston Blakely's home.

I'd barely turned, though, when flashing lights grabbed my attention from in the distance. As I drove closer, I could see police cars—one blocking my side of the road with a cop directing me to go around and two other police cars blocking an accident. Several inches of snow already covered the vehicles, but it was impossible to miss the cube van at an odd angle in a deep ditch. The back door was open, and I could just make out Detective Reinhart near the driver's-side door. I hoped the driver was okay. At least Detective Reinhart was on the scene. He was the most senior and competent detective on the force. If anyone could figure out who had run into the cube van and taken the clock, he could.

Sheila's tapping on the side door of my car made me realize how much I'd slowed and how anxious she was to get to her dad's house. We rode mostly in silence, with only Sheila's directions and whispers of "I can't believe it," punctuating the way. We drove a few miles out of town, and then she pointed me into a development of small townhomes with a sign that read: WELCOME TO BRECKENDALE RIDGE.

The houses were not extravagant. Certainly not mansions like the one Amber lived in. I guess I'd expected something fancier from the owner of an entire outlet mall. I wove down winding roads as Sheila directed me through the complicated development.

"Can you at least text your mom and just double-check that it's okay for you to spend the night?" I asked. At Amber's scowl, I added, "Of course, it's fine with me. I love having you over. I just want to make sure I'm not getting into any extra hot water with your mom."

Amber let out a scoff and sigh mixed together. "You're being ridiculous." But thankfully, she pulled out her phone, and it lit up from the backseat.

Finally, we reached a stretch of the development that was still under construction, or would be this spring. Neon property markers stuck up through the snow, indicating where new houses had been planned but not constructed yet. At the end of a cul-de-sac, there was one fully finished house.

"That's your father's house?" I drove toward it when she nodded, but for some reason, I still had a hard time believing it.

As if she could read my mind, she told me, "I told him he wouldn't be happy here. It's a far cry from where he used to live in Juniper Mills, believe me." Her last word caught in her throat, as though she was just remembering he would no longer be living anywhere.

I'd used to do that in the days and weeks after Cooper died—momentarily forget about the tragedy and then have to relive it again.

I pulled up along the curb and pulled out my phone to text Alex that we were here. Alex's unmarked police cruiser was parked in the driveway. There was an ambulance and one other unmarked police car along the curb.

"Are you sure you want to see him tonight?" I asked gently. It was nearly one in the morning, and she had to be exhausted.

Sheila nodded, resolute. "I have to." She got out on her side right as Alex's reply came through.

~I'll meet you at the front door of the house.~

"Do you want to stay here?" I asked Amber over the back of the seat. "I can leave the keys so you can stay warm."

I couldn't imagine her saying yes, but when a dead body was involved, as a responsible adult, I had to give her the option. In truth, she could probably handle this sort of tragedy better than I could.

Her only answer was to reach for her door handle.

When Amber and I got out, Sheila had circled the front of my car and was looking up. "I guess the power came back on."

Sure enough, there were three illuminated streetlights within the cul-de-sac—one right at the base of Winston Blakely's driveway. Without them or any other inhabited houses at this end of the subdivision, I could see how a person would want to get a generator going right away if they lost power.

Sheila headed for the side of a two-bay garage, but I stopped her with, "Detective Martinez said to meet him at the front door." She hesitated, and I had the impression she was about to ignore my words when lights brightened the upper floor of the house. Only seconds later, a front porch light came on. "Come on," I encouraged her. "Let's see what he has to say."

She only hesitated for one more second and then followed my lead toward the front door.

"I'm glad you're here," Alex said as he opened the door. If I'd thought he sounded tired, it was nothing compared to how he looked. His hair stuck up at messy angles, and he had dark circles under his eyes. His plainclothes detective uniform looked as though he'd been sleeping in it for the last month.

"This is Sheila Blakely." I motioned to her. I wasn't sure if I had mentioned her state of pregnancy on the phone, but Alex, the trained professional, showed no surprise. "This is Detective Martinez."

"I need to see my dad." Sheila's gaze darted behind Alex in the house and then back outside toward the garage.

"We'll do that." Alex's deep voice held an abundance of authority. "For now, though, let's allow the medical examiner to do his job while I ask you a few questions inside."

Chapter Five

A KETTLE WAS ON the stove of the small kitchen on the upper floor of the two-story house. I grabbed it, filled it with water, and set it to boil. The least I could do was make tea. Amber, on the other hand, was already seated beside Sheila with her notepad and pen out as though this was an investigation she had to solve.

"Now, is there anyone else living at this address, to your knowledge?" Alex asked.

Now that he'd asked, I saw a few feminine bits of décor around the kitchen—a tea towel on the stove handle with a flower bud attachment, lavender-scented hand soap behind the sink.

Sheila glanced away from Alex as she answered. "Jackie Reed. But she won't be here this weekend." Alex pressed her in who the woman was, and her jaw tightened before she said, "Dad's gold-digger girlfriend from Las Vegas."

"And do you know of her whereabouts right now?" Alex clicked his pen, ready to make a note. He never wanted a next of kin or roommate to wander into the tragic aftermath of a sudden death before he'd had time to explain if he could help it.

Sheila shrugged. "Who knows. Probably back with some boyfriend at a casino. If anyone told me, I wasn't listening." Alex made note of her words, but I guess during the pause, Sheila felt as though she had to fill the silence. "She won't care, by the way. Of if she does, she'll only care about his money.

But to be honest, I think my dad was too smart to leave her much."

What I thought was a purely distraught daughter of a deceased man quickly morphed before my eyes into a woman with a lot of anger and bitterness.

"How well do you know Jackie Reed? How long has she been in your father's life?" Alex asked.

The water started boiling so I looked for tea in the upper cupboards. I came up with a lovely ornate floral teapot, a matching sugar bowl filled with cubes, and four mismatched teacups.

"Dad met her last summer when he took a trip to Vegas. She didn't waste any time getting him to buy a place here and move in, but she often took off on weekends. Dad probably thought she was going to some spa—she always returned with freshly painted nails—but Dylan and I suspected she had another boyfriend on the side she was sneaking off to be with. Someone closer to her age."

"And when was the last time you spoke to her?"

I delivered the tea. Alex and Amber kept their eyes on Sheila, but she thanked me and proceeded to take a sip before answering. "It's been at least a month. I avoid coming by when she's here."

"Do you have a cell phone number for her, by any chance?" Alex took a sip of his own tea. Poor guy must have been more than ready for bed before I'd called him about Winston Blakely.

Sheila scoffed at this, which Alex assumed to mean no. But she at least seemed willing to help. "If you need to get a hold of her, just find Dad's cell. He has everyone in there."

"You said Jackie was away often?" Alex confirmed. "So can I assume you were over visiting often?"

Sheila nodded. "Almost every weekend. I just hoped to go into labor on a weekend because I really did not want Jackie at the hospital meeting my new baby while I was too exhausted to do anything about it."

It sounded to me like Winston did what he liked and wouldn't have kept Jackie away from visiting the hospital, even if he knew how much Sheila disliked her.

"And how long had your dad lived here?"

"Only six months. He moved to be closer to me and the baby."

Only a minute ago, she'd made it seem as though this Jackie Reed woman had forced him to move to Honeysuckle Grove. But if Alex had taught me anything, it was that grief often muddled people's answers, especially while they were still experiencing shock.

This answer made sense to Alex, and he quickly got back to the circumstances of Winston's death. "Was it common for him to start the generator? Did the power go out often?"

She shook her head. "Never to my knowledge. If I hadn't known he was supposed to be at the auction tonight, I wonder how long it would have been until someone found him." This sudden thought seemed to spike Sheila's emotions anew. She pulled out a tissue and wiped her teary eyes.

Alex had placed his phone on the table, faceup, and just then it lit up with a new text. He read it and then said, "We can go out there now if you like?" His most gentle voice had returned. When she nodded, he added, "I'll just have to ask you not to touch anything, Miss Blakely. Not even your father."

Chapter Six

As Amber and I waded through the knee-deep snow out the back door, Sheila barely seemed to notice it, on a mission to get to the cabin thirty feet in front of her in the back woods. If not for the bright police lights Alex had already set up, I wouldn't have even known a cabin was out here.

"That's his office?" I asked. It seemed hard to imagine for a mall owner.

Sheila nodded. Her boot stuck in the snow, and I rushed up ahead to the best of my ability to help her out of it. "Dad likes—liked to be away from everything when he worked."

Alex was in front of us and opened the cabin door. Winston Blakley was folded over, facedown on his large oak desk, his arms splayed out in front of him as though he was simply taking an uncomfortable nap.

The office wasn't large—about the size of my kitchen at home, and the desk took up the majority of it. Between the medics and medical examiner, as well as Alex and Sheila, there wasn't a lot of extra room, so Amber and I huddled together in the cold open doorway.

"Dad?" Sheila called, getting close to his face but obediently not touching him. Her voice still held hope, as though she somehow expected all the people in the room to have simply missed a regular pulse. "Dad?" she said again.

I wished I wasn't here for this part—the realization of the truth. It didn't seem to matter how long it had been since

Cooper's death, seeing this reaction in another person always brought it back in a visceral way.

Alex had a whispered conversation with the medical examiner. His name was Bob. I'd never heard a last name from the white-haired man, and I wasn't sure if calling him by his first name was appropriate, and so after seeing him at several crime scenes, I'd yet to have a conversation with the fatherly-looking, white-haired man. Another officer was taking photos of the generator, which had been unplugged and sat in the office near the door.

Alex moved closer to Sheila and placed a hand on her shoulder. "It's fine. Dr. Shone says it's okay if you want to touch your father." I was glad to finally have a last name for the medical examiner.

She touched her dad's shoulder as Alex let go of hers. She squeezed, and then she moved in closer to touch his face. She slid an arm around him and suddenly let out a wail of a cry, calling, "Daddy, no!"

When the truth of Cooper's death finally settled in on me, it had been a week after the fire. I'd been digging in my freezer for some hash browns and had come across a packet of frozen peas. I'd never been a fan of peas, but Cooper had loved them. I'd thought he was joking when he first told me—I mean, who loves *peas?*—but when I'd come to the realization that he was telling the truth, I'd started cooking them with a meal at least once a week. Finding the frozen peas and knowing I'd never make them for Cooper—that had been the thing that had gotten into my subconscious that he was really dead and never coming back. I'd collapsed right there beside the deep freeze.

Watching Sheila finding this revelation about her father so quickly, I felt awful for her loss, but I also experienced something strangely like jealousy.

Sheila pawed over her father for a few minutes, alternately trying to find some life in him and then giving up to her cries once again. Alex and Bob Shone returned to their quiet conversation, as though the woman's grief was nothing beyond the pain of losing a card game. I hoped I never became so used to people experiencing the death of loved ones.

"Do you want to wait in the house?" Amber asked. If I was uncomfortable with the display, I couldn't imagine what it was doing to Amber.

I told Alex where we were going and then led the way back across the snowy backyard. "And you should probably update your mom."

Amber scowled. "I'm sure she's sleeping. She hasn't texted back. Besides, I told you, she didn't want me there." This time, now that we were alone, hurt leaked out in her voice. She'd been too good at hiding it earlier.

My biggest problem was not knowing what I could say to make her feel better. "I'm sure it wasn't that she didn't *want* you there, Amber. It's her first New Year's without your dad. I'm sure she'll be back to her old self tomorrow. You'll see."

Amber raised an eyebrow and didn't bother retorting that her mother's recent "normal" wasn't much to look forward to.

After half an hour and another cup of tea, Amber looked at me across Winston Blakely's kitchen table and said, "Feeling better? Should we go back over?"

That was when I realized Amber thought she was rescuing *me* from the stress of the situation. The worst part was that she probably wasn't wrong in doing it.

We were just about to return to the cabin when Alex delivered Sheila Blakely back into the house.

"Do you mind getting Miss Blakely home?" Alex asked me.

I shook my head. "Of course not. I'd be happy to." I did have to wonder where the husband or boyfriend of this very pregnant woman was as she endured such heartache. "Just lead the way."

Alex told me he'd call me in the morning, and I had to admit, even if I wasn't glad for Mr. Blakely's early demise, I was certainly glad Alex felt like he had a reason to call me.

Chapter Seven

ALL THE WAY TO my car, Sheila kept shaking her head and telling me, "I can't believe this." It was a normal response, and there wasn't much you could say to alleviate the shock.

On the drive from her father's place, I held the bulk of the conversation, telling her about losing my husband a year ago. She murmured a couple of questions about funerals, clearly naïve about such things, as she didn't know how long to wait to hold it or what the funeral home would and wouldn't take care of.

"Once you've had a little rest, call me anytime, and we can work through the details together." I was earnest in my offer. It sounded as though Winston Blakely had not been married to this Jackie Reed, and if Sheila had her way, her dad's mistress shouldn't even be allowed at the funeral, which would leave Sheila, an only child, the sole person to make arrangements for her father.

"Please, don't hesitate to call me if there's anything I can do to help," I told Sheila as I pulled up outside the small, dilapidated townhouse Sheila had directed me to. At least the front walk had been shoveled, so she would have a much easier time getting to her house than she had to her father's office. I looked up at the dark townhouse. "Do you want me to come in with you?"

She shook her head. "No, that's okay. My boyfriend will be sleeping, and I don't want to wake him."

She didn't want to wake her poor sleeping boyfriend right after her father's death? But it wasn't my place to challenge this.

She thanked me and then headed up the short front walk toward her townhouse. As soon as she was inside and an interior light came on, Amber hopped into the passenger seat, and I backed out of the driveway.

"I can't believe she didn't even feel she could call on her boyfriend right after her dad died. She doesn't even feel like she can wake him up?"

Amber shrugged, her reaction to pretty much everything. "Everyone's different with grief. Maybe she knew her boyfriend would have a callous attitude about it."

I didn't think Amber had experienced that kind of callousness in her family, but the quick reasoning made me wonder if I was wrong. Thinking of her family brought me back to her mom.

"You're sure your mom wouldn't want you home tonight, after everything that's happened?"

She looked out her passenger window. "Look, if you don't want me to stay over, just say so." I'd never heard Amber so snarky toward me. Then again, she must have been exhausted. I certainly was.

"It's not that—" I started, but she wouldn't let me finish.

"If you're so worried about getting into trouble, just drive me home." She slumped back into her seat. "I'll have a better sleep in my own bed anyway."

I had no idea if this was true, but I drove up the mountain toward her mansion anyway. Every time she slept over at my place, she was up super early, not being able to sleep longer. I'd assumed it to be the same for her at home. But maybe not.

"Look, Amber, I always want you around," I tried comforting her. "I'm just worried about your mom. It seems out of character for her to want you out of the house, and I wonder if you might have read things wrong."

Amber scoffed and didn't reply, and we drove the rest of the way uphill to her mansion in silence.

Surprisingly, I had barely turned onto her street when I saw the lights from her mansion. It was almost three o'clock in the morning, and all the windows were illuminated as though it was barely dinner time.

"Was your mom expecting company?" I asked.

Amber didn't answer me directly and instead asked her own question. "What's Terrence Lane's car doing here?"

I'd met Terrence Lane the day I met Amber. He was a lawyer who had worked with Amber's dad at the law firm. He'd seemed shady at first, and at one point, I'd even suspected him of being responsible for Amber's dad's death.

I sucked in a breath, feeling even more concerned. I pulled in beside Terrence's navy Lexus in the driveway and put my car into park. In an instant, I decided not to offer Amber a choice about the matter. "I'm coming in with you."

She scowled, but didn't argue, which told me that maybe she was worried, too. At least a little.

Still, always bullheaded and filled with determination, Amber strode quickly up the cleared walk to her front door. She had the key code punched in and the door open by the time I got there. We walked in and immediately heard loud Top 40 music.

"Is your brother having a party?" I whispered to Amber. I bent to take off my boot, but as I did, Helen Montrose let out a loud laugh from the front room, which stopped me. I stood back up. She clearly hadn't done anything to hurt herself. But by the look on Amber's face, I could tell there was nothing normal about this situation.

"Mom?" she called, her voice unsure.

A second later, Helen Montrose came around the corner to the entry with her arm slung around Terrence Lane's shoulder. Terrence was tall and skinny, all angles and corners, and it couldn't be comfortable using him as a leaning post.

However, by Helen's bleary eyes, I suspected she didn't have her thoughts on comfort as much as remaining upright.

"Oh! Amber!" Helen turned to slur more words up to Terrence. "Look, Terrence, it's my baby girl."

I had thought Terrence was sober, or at least soberer than Helen until he started talking in his own slurred tongue. "I thought you said you got your kids out of here for the night." He spoke as if Amber, an impressionable sixteen-year-old, wasn't even here. His tone could only be described as a sneer. But I supposed she had been through worse.

In an instant, I made a decision and changed tacks. "Amber just forgot her toothbrush. We stopped by to get it."

A look of thankfulness crossed Amber's face. There was no way I would leave her here to take care of her drunk mother and the lawyer she'd decided to party the evening away with. They didn't need to know that Amber had had her own toothbrush at my place since the first time she spent the night.

"Oh, okay." Helen looked between me and Terrence. Terrence furrowed his brow into a scowl. "Well, hurry along then, honey." Helen motioned to the stairs.

Amber left her boots on and took the stairs two at a time toward the upstairs bathroom. She was back in an instant, toothbrush in hand, but during that time, Helen, Terrence, and I all stared at each other blankly, not knowing what else to say.

Helen wore pink lipstick and her usual bouffant hairstyle, but her hair had lost its normal pristine perfection, and her lipstick was smudged. She was also dressed up in a red sparkly dress. Terrence wore a suit, but his jacket was off, and his white shirt was rumpled. I wondered if we had interrupted a make-out session between them. And was this a serious development or only another outpouring of grief?

As soon as Amber was back down the stairs, Helen left her leaning post, pulling her arm away from Terrence, and made her way to her daughter. "Okay, well, you have a good sleep, honey. I'll see you tomorrow!" Her voice was too bubbly, and by the way she guided her daughter toward the door, it was as though she couldn't get Amber and me out the door fast enough.

Amber sighed. "Yup. See you." During the entire interaction, Amber had not acknowledged Terrence even once.

Before the door shut behind us, I heard Terrence asking Helen, "Who is the woman? Is she an aunt or something? Why's Amber out with her in the middle of the night?"

Great. Helen already thought it was strange that her daughter spent so much time with me. Now, apparently, her new boyfriend, or whatever he was, would only be fueling that fire.

Chapter Eight

I DIDN'T SLEEP IN often, so it surprised me when I looked over at my alarm clock the next morning and it was already eleven a.m.

I sat up quickly in bed, giving myself a bit of a head rush. Then again, it had been a long time since I'd been awake until four a.m. I wasn't a teenager anymore.

Thinking of teenagers, I strained to hear if Amber was awake and surprisingly heard whispered voices from downstairs. Was she talking on the phone? Had she called to demand answers from her mom about Terrence Lane? Or was she having a full-fledged conversation with my cat? Honestly, it would not have surprised me.

If we were talking about anyone else, I'd have no doubt in my mind that tearing a strip off her mom would have been her first agenda item for the day, but with her mom, Amber seemed to back off more than she confronted. I wondered if that had been normal practice before her dad had died or if it was new. I'd only known Amber from after her dad was gone, so I couldn't tell.

Finally, I decided to push myself out of bed, pull on a bathrobe, and make my way downstairs to check on the situation. I rounded the corner into the kitchen and stopped short. Alex sat across the table from Amber. She had Hunch on her lap, and all three of them leaned in to have a whispered conversation. In the seconds that it took them to notice me, my mind raced through my bedhead, my robe, and finally the details of what had transpired last night.

"Oh, good, you're up," Amber said at normal volume. "Alex made coffee, and there's fresh Danishes in the oven." She barely spared me a glance, and then she returned to focusing on Alex, who took one glance at me and then seemed embarrassed on my behalf and looked away. My cat didn't spare me the time of day, which was pretty normal when Amber was here.

"Um, great." My gaze darted around my kitchen. "I'll just... be right back."

I retreated backward out the door, and as I did, I heard Amber ask Alex, "So do you think it's serious?"

I wondered if she had told him the whole sordid story about her mother and Terrence Lane. I hoped so. Alex tended to give great parental advice where Amber was concerned. I was tempted to slip back into the kitchen to take part in the conversation, but vanity won out, and I raced up the stairs to change.

Five minutes later, I arrived back in my kitchen in jeans, a T-shirt, and with hair that had at least had a brush through it. I didn't look great, but at least I looked human.

Surprisingly, Alex and Amber still spoke in hushed voices, even though they knew I was awake. I supposed maybe she didn't want to speak too loudly about the Terrence situation.

But as I reached into the oven to retrieve a raspberry Danish for myself, Amber said, "So she's saying she thinks there was some kind of foul play? Do you think her suspicion is valid?"

I turned with my empty plate. "Foul play? What did he do?" My mind raced through last night's encounter with Terrence, how Amber's mom had been hanging off him. And now she was saying he had done something underhanded?

Alex turned to me. "It might be more about what he didn't do. Sheila is convinced that her dad would not have hooked up the generator inside his office. She says he knew better."

As he turned back to Amber, I tried to reset my mind onto the subject at hand. They were talking about the death of Winston Blakely, not about Amber's mother.

Alex went on. "In my experience, people enduring grief often grasp at straws, as they don't want to believe in a senseless and tragic outcome. All evidence leads me to believe he did hook up the generator inside his office. Perhaps he only meant to run it a short time. I could imagine it would have gotten cold in there quickly with the power out. Maybe he didn't realize how quickly carbon monoxide would fill the room and knock him out."

"And by the time you found him, he might have been in the small, contained room with plenty of gas for hours."

Alex nodded at Amber's input. "Carbon monoxide is odorless, but when I first opened his cabin door, the effect of it made me woozy and nauseated almost immediately."

"You've explained this to Miss Blakely?" Amber asked.

I finally turned and reached for my Danish. Even just picking it up, I could tell there was nothing store-bought about these pastries. Danishes were not a quick item to bake.

"How long have you been up this morning?" I asked Amber. "These smell amazing."

I grabbed coffee while Amber told me about the recipe she'd found in my recipe box—the box that contained my grandma's recipes, often her preference over my culinary school book. She explained the steps she'd taken in layering the pastry. It was her way of proving how much she'd learned from me in the kitchen.

"Amazing," I said again as I took my first bite. "You'll have to sleep over more often." In part, I said this to make up for the strange argument we'd had in the car last night and her thinking I didn't want her here. I also wanted her to know she always, *always* had a place to go if Terrence created an uncomfortable situation for her at home.

"What about the missing clock?" Amber asked Alex, her cheeks flushing from my praise. "Anything turn up with that?"

Alex shook his head. "Steve was the first one on scene. He lifted some prints from inside the cube van, but they haven't matched up with anyone with a record."

"What else was missing?" My brain was finally waking up enough to ask useful questions.

Alex sighed. "Strangely, there were several smaller and eas-ier-to-move antiques in the cube van, even expensive ones, and those went untouched. Even the jewelry."

"So do you think someone purposely ran the van off the road to steal the clock? But why? And how did they know it was in there?" Amber got jazzed up by the idea of anything mysterious. I had to admit, it was contagious when she asked these kinds of questions.

"That's what Steve suspects. Whoever did it would have needed their own truck or cube van to move the thing. It wasn't a small item."

"You should look into a man named Ted Callaghan." I thought back to the muscle-guy who had left right after the bidding ended for the clock. "Apparently, after his dad's death, the bank repossessed the clock. I'm pretty sure he was only at the auction to see who walked away with it."

Amber and I had spent the evening right next to the clock, which had loomed above both of us at probably eight feet high. I wondered how muscly Ted would have been able to move it on his own.

Alex made a note of the name.

"But the person who wanted that clock most, as far as we know, is now dead," Amber confirmed. "What are the chances?"

It was clear in Amber's tone that her mind was already reeling with possible tie-ins. I was still thinking—or at least hoping—there wasn't some big, orchestrated plan in this case. There had been a theft, for sure. But as far as I was concerned, it had nothing to do with Winston Blakely or his death—at least as long as Alex didn't find anything to prove otherwise.

Alex spoke as though we hadn't left the conversation of Winston Blakely. "I'm headed back to Breckendale Ridge shortly. I told Miss Blakely I'd have the forensics team thoroughly look over his office in the daylight, but I don't expect to find anything suspicious."

I sat at the table across from Alex. I would be glad to see a situation that didn't involve foul play. I'd been starting to fear Amber and I attracted that sort of thing. But not this time.

Or, at least, I hoped not.

Chapter Nine

I'D ALL BUT FORGOTTEN about New Year's Eve and the tragedy that had befallen Winston Blakely a week later when Sasha texted and invited me out with the lunch ladies the next afternoon.

~**Sure!**~ I texted back, hoping the brightness in my text would make up for the ambivalence I felt about it.

It wasn't as though I didn't enjoy Sasha's company, and I was sure I'd enjoy the other ladies as well. I guess I wasn't looking forward to all the preliminary questions. I'd have to talk about Cooper. I'd probably wear that "niceties" mask that was automatic with strangers, the one that had all but completely fallen off around Amber and Alex. I'd finally gotten comfortable being myself with them, and the two of them really felt like enough for me to open myself up to.

But I dutifully dug through my closet the next day and picked out a nice lunching outfit, trying to tell myself it was a good opportunity, and you never knew what kinds of things you could open your mind up to when getting to know new people.

But my other problem was what to tell Amber. She had the week off school for Christmas break, and her brother had been dropping her off every afternoon this week on his way to work so we could cook together. I told myself I shouldn't feel guilty for making plans one afternoon during the entire week. But I still felt it.

I'd planned to text her a few minutes before I headed out and let her know about my lunch, so it would be too late for her to ask if she could come along. Amber had been through a lot with her emotionally unstable mother, and even though she covered her rejection issues pretty well, I knew they were there, and I certainly didn't want to add to them.

I tried to plan my words carefully, but before I had a chance to text, my phone rang in my hands as I was running back upstairs to pick out some shoes and a purse.

"Hello?" I said, out of breath.

"What's wrong?" Amber said into the line. "You sound awful."

In an instant, I decided this might make a better excuse. No need for her to feel rejected if there were no other friends involved. Maybe I was simply under the weather. "Yeah, I'm not great," I agreed.

"Too bad. I just found some jumbo shrimp in our freezer. I thought we could make coconut shrimp again."

Coconut shrimp did sound delicious. But I'd already made plans, and now that I'd given my excuse, I figured I'd better stick with it. "Maybe tomorrow?" I suggested.

She sighed. "Yeah, okay. Whatever." I thought she'd hung up without saying goodbye, as she often did, but when I was about to hang up, she added, "Hope you feel better."

I tried to shake my regret over lying to Amber as I drove over to Sasha's house to pick her up. Sasha Mills was the only person over thirty I knew without a driver's license, and I found it humorous that Amber would likely have her license before Sasha.

"Do you think you'll ever drive?" I asked her as I drove us across town to Monica's Café, which I'd heard good things about but had never visited.

She shrugged. "Probably not. I have my life in Honeysuckle Grove figured out, and besides, it's good as a single person to have to go out of my comfort zone and ask others for help once in a while."

The idea sat with me through the entire drive. Sasha Mills had never been married. It made me sad that she seemed to have no hope of ever being anything other than a single person. She was pretty enough, but there probably weren't a lot of singles her age in Honeysuckle Grove.

The waitress—Carla, by her name tag—pointed us to a back corner of the restaurant where a few of the five ladies seated looked familiar, but I didn't think we'd ever officially met. They were all very chatty until we arrived at the table and Sasha made the introductions.

Barbara, Shelly, Rhonda, and Lea were all around Sasha's age. I took a seat beside the only person close to my age, Yvette, who I quickly deduced was Lea's daughter.

"I've seen you working with the kids on Sunday mornings," Yvette said. She wore jeans and a bright yellow sweater that looked great against her black hair.

I was often too busy corralling children to take note of parents coming and going. Sasha was most often in charge of that part because she knew them all well. "Right, right," I said, as though she was just as familiar to me. "Which kids are yours again?"

"Tommy and Tillie," she said. I knew Tommy well, as he had bitten more than one child in the preschool class. Tillie, I wasn't so sure about until she added her full name. "I mean Mathilda."

"Oh, yes!" I said. Mathilda wasn't as much of a bully, but getting her to sit through story time was always a hurdle. "They must keep you busy."

She agreed with this sentiment, and then she and Lea launched into several stories about the amount of work involved in raising twins. The other ladies at the table were all apparently grandmothers and had plenty of stories about their own grandkids.

I could certainly see why Sasha had been persistent in inviting me along, being the only one here without kids or a husband—as husbands came with their own ensuing plethora of stories. No one asked me about Cooper or my own child-rearing situation, which made me wonder if Sasha had tipped them off ahead of time.

I didn't mind sitting back and listening to their animated chitchat. It was enjoyable not to have the conversation focused on me and my late husband.

There was one spare chair at our table, which I figured wouldn't get used, but then the front glass door swung open and in swept Donna Mayberry, all long legs and bright red, rhinestone-flecked nails. There were a few off-putting things about Donna, like her gossiping tendencies, but I was thankful for her presence, if nothing else for her lack of kids.

"Mallory?" she asked as a question after greeting everyone else by name.

"Donna, hi!" I sat up straighter and donned my peppiest mask. "So nice to see you!"

Donna picked up the empty chair and brought it to my end of the table. She nestled it between mine and Yvette's chairs without any pause to see if it was okay. Yvette was quick to move hers aside. It made sense that Donna may want to sit at the younger end of the table.

But the second she was seated, she turned to me and said, "What have you heard about that stolen grandfather clock?"

I nibbled my lip to hold in my laughter. Of course, Donna wasn't interested in sitting with the younger crowd. She was interested in who had the most intriguing information to dish about.

But in this case, it wasn't me. "I'm afraid I can't tell you anything. Last I heard, Detective Reinhart was on the case, but I don't know any more than that."

Thankfully, Donna didn't seem to have gotten wind of Winston Blakely's death, or surely, she'd interrogate me all afternoon since I had actually been at the scene.

Donna raised an eyebrow. "So then tell me, what *is* happening with you and Steve Reinhart?"

The one time I'd gone out for dinner with Steve, it had actually been in an effort to nudge along a promotion for Alex. Unfortunately, Donna and Marv had been having dinner at the same restaurant that evening. This was not the first time she'd asked me about our date, but all I was able to tell her was the same thing I'd said the last time.

"We only went out that once. He was very nice, but I just didn't feel ready to date yet, you know, after Cooper." The second it was out of my mouth, all eyes at the table darted to me. I'd inadvertently brought up my late husband all on my own.

A full round of Head Tilts of Pity greeted me from around the table. In truth, I was feeling more and more ready to date these days. Unfortunately, the only person I would consider going out with was too busy to focus on a relationship. I'd told myself many times that this was the universe's way of offering me a little extra time to heal. But part of me was starting to feel anxious about it.

That anxiousness was probably what made me open my mouth to say, "Besides, if I wanted to date anybody, I think I'd be more interested in Detective Martinez."

Well, if nothing else, I'd assaulted the Head Tilts of Pity. Now everyone stared at me with glints of excitement in their eyes.

"Alex?" Donna asked, sounding equally excited. "I thought you were only helping him with investigations?"

I felt the sudden need to backtrack. After all, Alex and I should first discuss this with each other. The last thing I wanted was for my thoughts to get back to him via Donna's gossip posse. I waved a hand. "Oh, I am. I'm just saying *if*

I wanted to date anybody." My words didn't seem to quell anyone's excitement. Sasha was the only person at the table who I'd opened up with a little about my complicated feelings on the subject, and thankfully, she only offered a tight-lipped smile to the conversation.

I could feel a barrage of additional questions lining up on Donna's tongue, so I was thankful when our waitress reappeared with water and menus for everyone.

Looking at a menu gave me a chance to catch my breath and reset my mind on delicious food. Besides, diverting attention to culinary flavors was one thing I was adept with.

"I assume everyone's eaten here before? What do you recommend?"

The conversation became much more relaxed after that. Alex and Steve Reinhart were all but forgotten, and the soup of the day—a tortellini and Italian sausage mix—was something I'd come back for, if not try to recreate at home.

I left with a smile on my face and a promise that I'd try to join them again the next month.

And I would. Probably. I'd just have to keep reminding myself that getting comfortable with new people took time.

Chapter Ten

I'D COMPLETELY FORGOTTEN ABOUT my lie to Amber until I drove around the corner onto my street and saw her leaning beside my front door. I slowed and quelled my smile, my mind racing for what I could say to make up for my lie. I was clearly dressed up in a navy sweaterdress and had gone out *somewhere.* I wasn't going to be able to pile lies on top of lies with Amber, I knew that before I'd even put my car into park.

"Feeling better?" She raised an eyebrow as I tentatively got out of my car. "I brought homemade soup."

I sighed and went to unlock the front door. I motioned for her to go ahead, but she didn't seem willing without an explanation first. I sighed again. "Look, Amber, I didn't want to hurt your feelings or make you feel threatened in any way. You'll always be my best friend of anyone in this town."

She raised both eyebrows and made a rolling motion with her hand, like I should get on with the truth. So I did.

"Sasha Mills kept inviting me out for lunch with some local ladies. I felt bad that I kept turning her down."

Amber's forehead furrowed. "And so you lied about it...Why?" She sounded honestly confused, and I wondered if I'd been projecting my own insecurities onto her.

"I guess...well, I didn't want you to feel left out."

She laughed and finally led the way into my house. "From going out with a bunch of Miss Mills' old lady friends? I should thank you for saving me from that." I wasn't sure if I completely believed that Amber was this carefree about it, but before I could press her further, she changed the subject. "What'd you have for lunch?"

I cringed as I said, "Um... soup?"

She laughed under her breath and shook her head as she led the way to the kitchen. "More for me, I guess."

I followed, watching her carefully to see if she was truly so unbothered. Maybe her therapy sessions were doing wonders for her rejection issues. It reminded me that I wanted to make an appointment with her therapist—not only to talk about Cooper, but also to work through my lifelong struggle with my narcissistic father.

As Amber plugged in my slow cooker to warm her soup, my phone rang. I wondered if my dad had somehow sensed me thinking about him, but I didn't recognize the number so I picked up. "Hello?"

"Is this Mallory Beck?" I recognized the high-pitched woman's voice, but couldn't immediately place it.

"Yes. What can I help you with?"

"You told me I should call after getting some rest?" When I didn't immediately respond, searching my brain for what she was talking about, she added, "This is Sheila Blakely."

"Oh, right. Of course." In an instant, I dropped into a more somber tone. "Yes, I'm more than happy to help or to talk. Whatever you need."

Last I heard of Sheila Blakely, Alex had called to tell her there'd been nothing unusual at the scene of her father's death. There hadn't been any clear fingerprints on the generator, most likely because of the snow. Alex had relayed to me that she was still having a really hard time accepting that it had been an unfortunate accident, and she'd even gone over his head to Captain Corbett to request that another detective take a look.

Steve Reinhart had been the detective assigned to this, but he didn't find anything out of the ordinary either. I had slightly mixed feelings toward Sheila for this upheaval she'd caused at the police department—Alex's captain already held a personal grudge against him—but my compassion for a woman who had recently lost someone close won out.

"Yes, well, I have the funeral booked for next Friday, the fourteenth, at Sayward's Funeral Home. I think I have everything in order for it."

I nodded, wondering why she was calling if she'd already made all of the arrangements. Just to talk? When Cooper died, I was thankful to have his insurance settlement. The funeral director at Sayward's had talked me through every step of a very distressing and overwhelming process, but it hadn't been cheap. Now that I was clearheaded, I could see he'd likely talked me into several purchases I hadn't really needed. I was quite sure with Winston Blakely's wealth, Sheila would have been in a similar position. But then I recalled her dilapidated townhouse.

"If you'd like, I could go over it all with you, make sure there's nothing they sold to you that you don't really need."

"No, no. That's fine. Dad had it all planned with them, so I didn't have to make any decisions."

I squinted at her response. Winston Blakely had been sixty-three. Old enough, perhaps, to have thought to prepare his affairs in case something happened to him. But what were the chances he'd done that at the local funeral home during the short time he'd lived in Honeysuckle Grove?

I shook my head. There I went again, trying to stir up questions where there weren't any. "I'm glad," I told her. "So how can I help?"

"You said I should call about catering the food?"

I didn't think I had. In fact, Amber and I would have already planned a full menu and talked nonstop about it, if that had been the case. Perhaps Sheila had misunderstood my offer to help. It didn't matter. This was certainly something we could help with.

"We'd be happy to cater," I told her, watching an ecstatic reaction bloom on Amber's face. "What were you thinking of serving?"

When I had all the details, I had no sooner hung up when Amber let out an excited squeal. "See? I told you we'd be a success. And before we've even placed an ad!"

Amber dropped into a chair at my kitchen table and pulled out her laptop. As soon as it booted up, she turned her screen to show me an ad she'd been working on to put into the paper for our new catering business. She had superimposed a photo of the two of us into her ad, and it looked professional, other than the NAME PLACEHOLDER part, which highlighted the fact that we hadn't agreed on a name for our new business yet.

"Calm down." I kept my voice even. "We have to get a permit from the health department before we should do any advertising."

"We'll at least have the ad ready as soon as we can get a permit, and now we should have some glowing reviews to include as well!" Amber was constantly pushing boundaries or trying to fudge rules, so I was hesitant to allow this, but at the same time, I was probably as excited as she was at the prospect of starting a catering business together. Besides being able to cook alongside my best friend, it would give us a ready answer for anyone who thought it was strange that we spent so much time together. "I'll get working on a menu. I should be able to get it done before my therapist appointment."

As we'd cooked during the last week, Amber had brought up Terrence a couple of times, but there hadn't been a lot to share. He hadn't been around since New Year's Day, apparently, and when Amber brought him up to her very hungover mother, she had quickly changed the subject and asked Amber to clean the kitchen.

She had been alarmed at how many liquor bottles had been littering the kitchen counter, especially with her mom on so many meds, and had expressed her concerns to me. I suggested she bring it up with her therapist, so I was glad that was finally happening today. In truth, I wasn't sure what to do about Helen Montrose, or if anything needed to be done at all. It had just been a one-time event at this point.

But at least after today, a professional could help to make those decisions.

Chapter Eleven

THE NEXT FRIDAY, AMBER and I showed up at the funeral home just before noon for a one o'clock funeral. Sheila Blakely had requested a variety of sandwich quarters, along with vegetarian and gluten-free options, fruit and vegetable trays, and a mix of desserts that she left up to our discretion. Amber had had a field day with that kind of freedom, trying out at least three new baked goods each afternoon after school until we settled on a half dozen varieties.

I'd spent a fair amount of time at Sayward's Funeral Home last year, so I knew my way around enough to park near the back entrance and head straight down the stairs into the funeral's reception room.

The place was empty. It wouldn't take us long to drape tablecloths and set out the food, but the big coffee urn I'd just purchased would take a good half hour to heat, and I wanted to have everything ready so I could sneak upstairs and sit in on the service if there was room. Amber and I hadn't known Winston Blakely, of course, but it felt like part of my responsibility as the caterer to hold a conversation about the beauty and nostalgia of the service.

"Are you going to come upstairs?" I asked Amber at ten to one when everything was ready in the reception room. The dozen tables had been draped in tablecloths, and we had a fully stocked tea and coffee station along with an oblong food table that didn't hold an inch of free space.

She shook her head. "Nah. I'll watch over everything here."

I couldn't imagine anyone strolling downstairs and fiddling with our food trays during the service, but I figured it was more likely that Amber didn't have any desire to be near another funeral after the one recently held for her dad. Too many memories. I understood that, and yet during the last few months, I'd come to a place where I wanted to remember some of the details that were blurred from the haze I had been in shortly after Cooper's death.

"Sounds good," I told her and held up my phone. "Text me if you need anything, and I'll text you when it's time to take off the plastic wrap."

She nodded and slumped into a nearby chair with a game already open on her phone.

As I ascended the stairs, I wondered if they'd already closed the doors to the chapel, because it seemed unusually quiet up there. But as I reached the top step, I saw the doors were both propped open and all of five people were scattered within the chapel. Amber and I had prepared sandwiches and food for fifty at Sheila's request. I suddenly worried that I'd somehow gotten the time wrong.

Sheila sat on the front bench of the chapel, where there was an open casket five feet from her. She wiped her eyes with a tissue. Her boyfriend, Dylan, sat beside her, consumed with something on his phone. She wore a black dress that accentuated her large belly while he looked out of place next to her in jeans and the same blue plaid jacket he'd worn on New Year's Eve.

Because the place was so empty, I could make out most of the conversation when Soren Sayward, the funeral director, approached them.

"Are we still waiting for some additional guests?" He was better at hiding his surprise than me, but he still glanced around the chapel to highlight his concern.

Sheila looked back from the front row. Her eyes and nose were red. On instinct, I slipped into the last bench, as though I alone could somehow make the place look fuller.

"I don't know," she told him. "I thought people would travel to his new hometown to honor him, but I guess not."

"Honor him?" Dylan said under his breath and then let out a low chuckle. He didn't seem to care that his distaste for the recently deceased, a man his girlfriend cared deeply about, was obvious.

Sheila's eyes lingered on each of the other three people in the place. She dropped her voice, but it could still be heard all the way in the back of the echoey room. "I don't even know these people."

When her eyes settled on me, I felt uncomfortable, suddenly wondering if it was strange that a caterer who had never even met her dad had helped herself to a seat. I was about to stand and retreat—I could always feign some kind of food emergency downstairs—but then she met my eyes with a sad but genuine smile.

She turned to the funeral director to give the go-ahead for the service. I'd barely relaxed back into my seat when a tall blonde woman swept in through the back doors.

She couldn't have even been thirty, with bright yellow flat-ironed hair and a wrinkle-free face. She wore a leopard print dress with a matching purse and bright red lipstick that matched her wool overcoat. If anyone's appearance screamed Las Vegas, it was this woman's. This must be the lady Winston had been dating, Jackie Reed.

Sheila circled her hand toward Soren Sayward and said in an urgent, much louder voice, "Start the service. We need to start the service now!"

Dylan wasn't as quick to take his eyes from the vivacious woman. He pocketed his phone and stared back at her, but I sensed it was not attraction he felt toward her. Tension rose in the room as though a rubber band was stretched taut between them.

Soren Sayward was a master at defusing tension, though, and quickly took the podium on a small stage at the front. He wore a black suit that matched his hair and spoke in a voice that, despite its softness, could easily be heard from the rear of the chapel. "Thank you for joining us today as we remember Winston Alfred Blakely," he said far enough from the microphone that I doubted it was amplifying him.

A gasp sounded, and I looked over to see the blonde standing against the back wall, crying loudly into a tissue. Her outburst was so sudden, and she'd looked so composed walking in thirty seconds ago, that I figured her emotion had to be an act. A man with a beard sitting a row in front of her looked back. He wore a brown suit and kept his gaze on her for a strangely long time. I wondered if he knew her or just didn't have a clear handle on funeral etiquette.

Soren Sayward soon gathered the attention of the room again. One other man sat a few benches up from me. He didn't seem as interested in Jackie, but he also didn't seem terribly interested in the service. A man in his fifties with gray hair, he kept his gaze on his phone screen as Soren proceeded to read a long diatribe about Winston Blakely's life.

I took in the bullet points: He'd been a business owner since he left college in the seventies. He built his fortune from nothing before finally purchasing Juniper Mills Outlet Center in Juniper Mills, West Virginia. His wife abandoned him shortly after the birth of his one child, Sheila Blakely. Many might have referred to Winston as a cutthroat businessman, but his daughter only knew him as a loving and kind father.

The list of his accomplishments in business and investments went on, but by the time Soren finished up and asked if anyone cared to say a few words about Winston, there had been no mention of Jackie Reed.

Jackie didn't seem to miss this. Sheila hadn't had time to push herself up to a standing position around her pregnant belly before Jackie marched up the center aisle toward the podium. She had pulled herself together again, or at least I thought so until she made it behind the microphone, said one word, "Winston," and let out another loud round of hysterics. Unlike Soren, she held herself too close to the microphone, and her cries were amplified throughout the chapel.

The small group of us waited out her emotions while she collected herself and wiped her eyes. When she spoke, her voice seemed much more even than I expected.

"Winston was my true love, and I can't believe he's gone." Again, she spoke very close to the microphone, and her voice was louder than it needed to be with the small crowd. She didn't seem to notice. "He had a soft spot for me. We dreamed of seeing the world together. We had plans to open a new mall right here in Honeysuckle Grove." She shook her head, which gave me time to pause and remember the conflicting stories about why Mr. Blakely had moved to town. At first, Sheila had indicated that Jackie had forced him to, then she said he'd moved here to retire closer to his grandchild. Now Jackie was saying they agreed to move here to open a new mall? "I don't know what I'll do without my Winnie."

Sheila openly scoffed at this nickname. She'd finally gotten herself to a standing position, and she hadn't bothered to sit again through Jackie's speech. In fact, she started to make her way up onto the small platform where the podium stood, as though she might just push her father's mistress out of her way.

Jackie nibbled her lip and broke down in tears again. Sheila crossed her arms atop her large belly, and Jackie must have seen her out of her peripheral vision because she left the platform in the other direction, wiping her eyes as she went.

"My dad, *Winston* Blakely," Sheila said in a curt voice, "was a no-nonsense man. He had made some enemies, for sure, and didn't always rub people the right way, but he was my dad, and

I knew him better than anyone. He didn't have *soft* spots. He was a hard man, and yet I always knew he loved me."

Sheila continued, but as she did, I glanced over my shoulder. Jackie had silently made her way out of the chapel and out of the building. As Sheila went on, her voice became less angry and hard, I suspected because she no longer felt as though she had to prove anything to Jackie Reed.

Following Sheila's words, Soren Sayward took to the microphone again. "Would anyone else like to say anything about Winston Blakely?"

Dylan was on his phone again and didn't seem to hear the question. The other two men in the chapel looked to me, but I had nothing to say. I gave my head a quick shake, and thankfully, Soren seamlessly ended the short and to-the-point service.

He had barely thanked everyone for coming and announced the reception downstairs when I was out of my seat and headed in that direction, texting Amber on my way.

A very strange service. And now Amber and I would have to figure out what to do with a boatload of leftover food.

Chapter Twelve

OF THE TWO GENTLEMEN from the service, only the younger one with the beard made his way downstairs. Both Amber and I smiled at him and told him to help himself, but he barely acknowledged us. He took two paper plates and heaped one with six sandwich quarters, and the other with spears of pineapple, mango—which had been expensive, as they were out of season—and three desserts.

Maybe we wouldn't have so much leftover food after all.

I was about to make pleasantries about the service with him, as he was the only guest to make his way downstairs so far, when he spun and turned the conversation on me.

"How did you know Blakely?"

I looked to Amber, as though she might have the answer. "Oh, I'm afraid I didn't. I met his daughter on New Year's Eve, the night of Mr. Blakely's death, and shortly afterward she asked if I would cater the funeral."

He raised an eyebrow. "Is it normal for a caterer to attend the service where she's only there to provide food?"

I was taken aback by his bold question, mostly because I hadn't gotten my footing with what was normal for a catering company yet. I decided coming clean might put this man's mind at ease. Or at the very least it might make me feel less awkward.

"I'm afraid this is only our second catering event. Our first was at an antique auction on New Year's Eve, so we're still learning the ropes." I motioned to Amber. I could tell by her single raised eyebrow that she didn't appreciate me lumping her in with my inexperience and putting it out there so plainly.

"You were at the auction?" The bearded man was in his early thirties. Some men with beards kept them trim and stylish, and in my mind, a beard added to their attractiveness. Not so with this man. He'd left his scruffy and untrimmed, and now that I saw him closer up, I noticed that even though he'd worn a suit to the service, there were frays along the wrists of the blazer. I wasn't quite sure, though, whether the disheveled look was due to a lack of affluence or simply a trend. It was hard to tell. His brown leather shoes, while also weathered, had fine stitching that indicated quality.

"Yes. Amber and I catered the event." Again, I motioned beside me to Amber, and this time, she didn't seem to mind the acknowledgment.

"So you were there for all the bidding?"

I suddenly felt as though I was being interrogated. On instinct, I turned a question back on him. "I'm sorry, how did you say you knew Mr. Blakely?"

"I didn't," he snapped. "Did you see the bidding?"

He didn't know Winston Blakely, yet he was here and very interested in the auction the deceased man had planned to attend? Something seemed fishy about this.

"I was in the community center during the bidding, yes," I told him slowly.

"So you saw who bid on the grandfather clock?"

I thought back. The evening of bidding had become a bit of a blur in my mind. Amber and I had spent several hours beside the clock, so I was familiar with the piece, but I couldn't recall particular bidders. Donna Mayberry had bid early on. I wasn't sure who else, except for Sheila, who had been bidding on her father's behalf.

"I'm afraid I couldn't tell you," I said.

Just then, Dylan's and Sheila's voices sounded near the bottom of the stairs, though I couldn't make out their words.

The bearded man heard them, too, glanced over his shoulder, and then turned back to me. "I gotta go."

"Mr...? I didn't get your name," I said as he swept past me, jostled past Sheila and Dylan, and was gone a second later.

Dylan headed straight for the food, and for a second time, I wondered if we hadn't prepared heaps too much. Amber went to rearrange the desserts as Sheila strode straight for me. I tore my eyes from the stairwell where the bearded man had disappeared and pasted on a caring smile.

"I'm so sorry," Sheila said. "I guess I overestimated the attendance. I was certain it would be a full house of people who had to see with their own eyes that he was gone."

It was an interesting turn of phrase. Sheila seemed to have made peace long ago with the fact that her dad wasn't terribly likable to others, even if he was her own personal hero.

"I wouldn't worry," I told her, motioning to Dylan. "Between your boyfriend and the last gentleman who was down here, there shouldn't be too much going to waste. Any idea who that gentleman was?" I recalled she'd mentioned not knowing the other attendees.

She didn't seem to hear my question and rubbed her belly. "Plus, I'm eating for two these days." She glanced over her shoulder toward Dylan and dropped her voice when she asked, "Did you bring me a bill?"

This was the uncomfortable part. I reached behind our prep table for my purse. At first, I'd told Amber that I planned to do the funeral pro bono, but Amber wouldn't have it. She'd said, "Mallory, if we're going to make this business work, we need to start how we plan to go forward. Do you think this business will survive if we're spending money on expensive food and then cutting deals for everyone?"

It had sounded like a spiel she'd learned from her dad, the lawyer. But when I'd nibbled my lip in worry about how much to charge Sheila, Amber had finally relented and said, "We have to at least charge for the food."

So that had been our compromise for this particular event. It was hard to explain the compassion I felt for Sheila and the palpable funeral stress I felt on her behalf. While Cooper had left me a great insurance settlement after his death, it had taken some time to have it pay out. In the meantime, I was swimming through a pool of grief and being charged through the nose for funeral expenses because I didn't know any better. I certainly did not want that same thing to happen to Sheila.

I passed over an unmarked envelope. She opened it right in front of me, adding to my discomfort. "What? This can't be it?"

I tilted my head. "Listen, after my husband's death, I know how difficult it can be. Between will readings and insurance settlements, nothing happens quickly. We wanted to give you a break." I motioned to Amber, even though we both knew I was only speaking on my own behalf.

"Oh, yes, well." She glanced at her boyfriend again. "Dad gave everything to that tramp of his, so I appreciate this. Don't worry, I'm contesting the will, though, and the judge has to see my side of things. I mean, Jackie hasn't even known him a year, and she was nowhere to be found the night of his death." She scoffed. "I'll certainly pay you your full rate when the dust settles."

"All that matters is that you feel like you've honored your dad today. I hope I've helped make the day a little less painful."

She assured me I had.

Even though I didn't know anyone in this family, something bothered me, too, about Winston's entire estate going to a woman he'd known less than a year. By the looks of Jackie Reed, she would have done well in Las Vegas as a showgirl or a cocktail waitress.

"You said Jackie was out of town the night your dad passed, right?" I couldn't seem to hold my question in.

Sheila nodded. "She must have just left. I told Dad we could go to the auction together, but he said he'd meet me there as soon as Jackie got on her way."

"What time do you figure that might have been?" The part of me that couldn't let go of the details surrounding a death was still focused on how long that generator must have been running for the fumes to have nauseated Alex the second he walked in.

Sheila's brow furrowed. "You know…" She drew out the word. "If Jackie was still home, maybe *she* set up the generator in his office. She's quite an airhead. That would make a lot more sense than Dad doing it. Do you think Detective Martinez thought of that?"

I was torn. Part of me thought this was a valid point. If Winston Blakely's entire estate was going to Jackie Reed, and she had been the last one to see him alive, what were the chances that she might have done something to hurt him—something that could look like his own accidental fault? At the same time, I didn't want to stir up any more suspicion in Sheila than I had already by bringing up the question, and I didn't want her to bother Alex, who was balancing his time between several cases these days.

"I might be able to mention it to him if you'd like." I wasn't completely sure if I meant this, as I didn't want to bother Alex with something that was probably nothing.

"Would you?" She smiled and tilted her head, but then I had the distinct impression she could read my indecision on the matter.

Instead of answering, I asked my own question. "What do you think about Miss Reed's suggestion that your dad wanted to open a mall in Honeysuckle Grove?"

Sheila shook her head. "I'm sure she came up with that harebrained idea to make their relationship somehow sound more serious or more permanent. Do you really think Honeysuckle Grove is big enough to support a mall?"

"I suppose not."

Thankfully, she changed the subject back to the spread of food. "Listen, I'll fill a plate for myself and then you ladies can feel free to pack up."

"The other gentleman isn't coming down for a bite?" I asked.

Her brow furrowed, but then understanding dawned on her. "Mr. Mahoney? Oh, no. He didn't stick around."

I was glad she at least knew the other attendee's name. From past experience, I knew Soren Sayward never joined in on the receptions. "Did you know the other gentleman who was here? The man with the beard?" I tried again, motioning to the doorway where he'd pushed past Sheila and her boyfriend.

She looked in that direction and took a moment to think it over. "He must be someone Dad knew through his many businesses over the years. I published the obituary in the Juniper Mills paper as well as the *Honeysuckle Grove Herald*, so he could be from either town."

That made sense. "He had a strong interest in the antique auction."

"Oh?" Sheila's attention was suddenly divided as Dylan motioned her over toward where he'd taken a seat to wolf down his large plate of sandwiches. "I should go sit with Dylan, but do feel free to pack up and go whenever you'd like."

I assured her we would. She helped herself to a plate of food, and then Amber and I packed up the rest.

As we left the building, Amber suggested we drop off the leftovers at the food bank. Even though my good intentions from today should have given me some sense of philanthropy, I headed home feeling like I hadn't done anything useful at all.

Chapter Thirteen

ALL EVENING, I COULDN'T shake the conversation I'd had with Sheila. Amber's mom had wanted her home, and I cleaned up my house, waiting for Alex's call. It was after eleven the next morning when it finally came.

"How was the funeral?" he asked as soon as I picked up and put him on speakerphone. His voice was gentle, as though he had some idea how much spending the day at a memorial of any kind, even for someone I didn't know, might bother me.

"Pretty empty." I filled a glass with juice and took it to my living room to talk. Hunch, my multiple-personality cat, followed me in there, hopped onto my lap, and immediately started purring, as though he thought he might find out some investigative details from our conversation if he acted nice enough. "Only a handful of people there, including me. Too bad we made enough food to feed an army. Don't worry, we saved you some."

"Heh, heh. Well, I might not make it by for any today, I'm afraid. I'm busy with Steve, probably until late. Plus, there are still extra details to look into with the Blakely investigation."

Now I felt extra bad when I asked, "Did Sheila Blakely call you again?"

He sighed. "Yes. She mentioned the two of you had been talking about Jackie Reed, and you thought I'd be interested in her suspicions." My face flushed at his words. Not only had she called, but she'd made it sound as though *I* had suggested she call? "I'm afraid I just don't have time to get over there and interrogate Jackie Reed ASAP—her words," he added.

"Pretty busy with Steve's case, huh?"

"Really busy. We've had a couple of leads open up, and they're time sensitive." This was about the most Alex had told me about the mysterious case he and Steve Reinhart were investigating together. Alex had been instructed in no uncertain terms not to share any information about this particular case with either Amber or me. I was trying hard not to be offended and not to pry.

"Plus, there's that stolen clock. Chad Wyatt from Chad's Antique Village and the buyer from the auction are both driving Steve crazy. Both are worried about being out the clock and the money. Apparently, Chad's insurance policy that should cover all the auction items has vague wording, and they don't want to pay out, and the bank that had taken ownership of the clock during a recent foreclosure is also concerned about the loss of funds. They're all driving Steve crazy, putting pressure on him to find that stupid clock, but we just don't have much to go on."

"Did you follow up on Ted Callaghan? He was the son of the previous owner of the clock," I reminded him.

"I've left a couple of messages, but so far he hasn't gotten back to me. If only I had the time to pay him a personal visit."

Part of me wanted to offer to take on that particular interview to help Alex out. But remembering Mr. Callaghan's muscular body and stern demeanor, I wasn't sure that was the safest place for me to show up alone.

"There was a bearded man at the funeral who was asking about the auction and specifically about who was bidding on the grandfather clock," I told him. "But Sheila didn't seem to know who he was." The moment it was out of my mouth, I realized this wasn't giving him much to go on. My mind scrambled for any other ways I might help. "Or what about Roland, the auctioneer? He left shortly after the cube van left with the antiques." I explained how grouchy the auctioneer had been toward anyone with means and regarding picking up his payment. As I said it, I realized it wasn't the strongest motive, but at least it was something. "I could go by Chad's Antiques and inquire a little more after Roland if you like?"

"That would be great, Mal. Really." Tiredness leaked out in his voice.

I wished there was some other way I could help. The moment another idea came to me, I spoke it. "What do you think about me dropping by to have a conversation with Jackie Reed, too? Just asking a few questions and laying the groundwork until you or someone else on the force has time for a thorough interview?"

Even though I couldn't see Alex, I could sense him nodding on the other end of the line. "Be careful. I don't think you should go alone, but I sure would appreciate the help."

Not going alone was his way of suggesting I take Amber along, without actually suggesting I put a sixteen-year-old on the case. Amber was wise and intuitive beyond her years, but Alex would still get a ton of flak if his boss knew he'd authorized a teenager to assist with an investigation. We knew this from experience.

"Maybe we'll even bring Hunch." I ran a hand over my temporarily loving cat, and a big part of me knew saying this aloud would be enough for Hunch to make sure he held me to it.

As soon as I got off the phone with Alex, I called Amber. It was Saturday, so she didn't have school. Even though she still had homework, as soon as I asked what she was up to, she assured me she'd much rather complete it at my place.

"Why? What's going on at home?"

She sighed. "Terrence. At least they weren't drunk last night, but Mom's so weird around him, like the giddy teenagers I went to middle school with. It's like she's completely forgotten about Dad and moved on."

"She probably hasn't," I assured her. "But grief can be weird. Suddenly, it might seem like doing something crazy might make the pain go away."

I didn't want to get into the time shortly after Cooper's death when I'd gone to a virtual arcade every evening for a week straight. The VR force and all the mental stimulation gave me a strange kind of break from my emotions for a few minutes. It was addictive—until six or seven days later when my mind adapted, and suddenly, I was bawling my eyes out behind my VR headset.

Amber didn't ask why I was inviting her over until her brother dropped her off. She showed up at my door with a backpack full of school books, took one look at my face, and said, "Oh. We're investigating?"

"When you're done." I motioned to her backpack, to which I received an exaggerated eye roll. Then she just stared at me until I relented. "Okay, but we won't be gone long, and you *have to* study the minute we get back."

Another eye roll, but I was pretty sure this second one indicated her agreement. I'd learned to read Amber's body language pretty well in the last six months.

We headed for my kitchen where I'd started on a Greek moussaka, one of my favorite hearty dishes.

"We're cooking first?" Amber guessed. She nodded. "Of course, we are."

"We have to pave the way for a casual interrogation," I told her and then instructed her to check the potatoes boiling on the stove for tenderness.

"And who are we interrogating, and what case are we talking about? Did Alex ask for our help on something?"

So many questions. But who was I kidding? I'd have just as many if she was the one in the know.

"Sheila Blakely wanted Alex to check into her father's mistress, Jackie Reed. Apparently, she is the sole heir to his fortune, and she was the last one to see the man alive. Sheila believes his mistress might have had reason and opportunity to move the generator that killed Winston Blakely into his office." I neglected to mention that I might have actually been the first one to plant this seed of suspicion in her mind and felt somewhat responsible to clear it up. "Alex is super busy with that case he's working on with Steve Reinhart."

This was the second topic in this short conversation that made me uncomfortable. I was peeling stripes down the sides of my eggplants and almost sliced a layer off my finger with a little too much pressure. I put the eggplant down and decided to finish this conversation first and peel after.

Thankfully, Amber didn't dwell on the case Alex was keeping private from us. "So we're going to question this Jackie Reed lady on Alex's behalf, see if she might have killed her boyfriend?" Before I could answer, she added, "And for some reason, you thought this Greek moose stuff would help pave our way?"

I nodded and picked up my next eggplant. Now that the topic was back on food prep, I could work and talk. "Moussaka. Initially, I considered a lasagna, but I had a sudden concern that Jackie Reed might be gluten free. Moussaka is thought of as a Greek lasagna." Amber looked at the ingredients on the counter and then raised an eyebrow back at me. "Because of the layers," I explained.

She drained the potatoes, and I had her layer them along the bottom of two casserole dishes—one for Jackie Reed and one for us.

"Why the stripes?" She motioned to the three eggplants I'd peeled stripes down and was slicing into half-inch rounds. "Just to make it pretty?"

I shook my head. "The skin can be tough, but it also adds a nice flavor. The peeling helps break it up on the plate, so you don't end up with large chunks of eggplant that are difficult to break apart."

She nodded and watched as I slipped the eggplant rounds into a brine to soak. Then I had her sauté a couple of yellow onions and add ground beef. As that started to brown, I pulled allspice, cinnamon, oregano, salt, and pepper from my cupboard.

"Allspice and cinnamon?" Amber asked with yet another raised eyebrow as she watched me pour teaspoons into the meat.

I smiled back at her. "You'll see."

Once the meat was browned, I taught Amber how to make the béchamel sauce, one of my favorites from when I worked at Baby Bistro in college. Back then, I'd always made it standard with whole milk and bread flour, but today we were making a low-allergen version with rice flour and my dairy-free half-and-half.

Once the layers of the moussaka were assembled, we sprinkled parmesan on top and then set it to bake for forty-five minutes. While we waited, we talked through the details surrounding Winston Blakely and Jackie Reed.

"She showed up at the funeral, swept in right at the last minute, and seemed perfectly fine. Then she had a sudden outburst of tears at the microphone. It seemed as though it could have been just for show."

Amber shrugged. "I don't know. It sounds a little like how my mom acted after my dad died."

She had a point. "Jackie also said something about the two of them planning to open a mall right here in Honeysuckle Grove. Sheila didn't seem to know anything about that, and she thought Jackie was making it up just to look like they had a more permanent relationship than they did."

"How old is this Jackie Reed lady?"

"I'd guess around my age."

Amber raised an eyebrow. "And she was dating a sixty-three-year-old?"

It did sound strange, and I couldn't see the appeal, but it was not unheard of for older wealthy men to take up with beautiful young women who wanted to be shown a nice time.

"So we'll question her about Mr. Blakely's will, and what she plans to do with the money?"

I made a note in my notebook. "And also where she was on New Year's Eve and what time she last saw Winston alive. I'd also like to know what kind of a mental and emotional state he was in when she left."

We hadn't seriously considered suicide, as Sheila hadn't found any merit in that theory, but perhaps his mistress saw angles his daughter didn't.

"Great," Amber said. "And, you know, whatever else comes up."

I agreed, and if I knew Amber, I suspected more would definitely come up—a brilliant question or two that hadn't even occurred to me.

Chapter Fourteen

I'D FORGOTTEN TO ASK Alex for any contact information for Jackie Reed, but I figured it would make sense to find the woman in the home she'd shared with Winston Blakely in Breckendale Ridge. When we drove through the maze of a subdivision, this time following my GPS, something looked different about Mr. Blakely's house at first glance.

A FOR SALE sign was now propped into the snow at the edge of the driveway.

"She's selling it already?" Amber asked the question that was on the tip of my own tongue.

"I guess. Wow, that didn't take long."

Thankfully, there were lights on in the upper floor of the main house, so it looked as though someone was home. There was also a Prius similar to mine in the driveway, but this one was red and the newest model.

I didn't want to have anything in common with this woman if she indeed had something to do with killing her wealthy boyfriend for his money, and so I parked out along the curb, instead of putting the two Priuses side by side in the driveway.

It was Saturday afternoon around three. I'd gotten Amber to work on some of her homework while the moussaka was baking, but it would be getting dark soon, and I was never as comfortable questioning a suspect after dark, even if I did have Amber with me. In truth, I'd had my life put in danger by suspected murderers more than once in the daytime, but the few horror movies I'd watched in my younger years left me with fears about what might lurk around dark corners.

Amber carried the moussaka, and I rang the doorbell. Seconds later, footsteps sounded descending the stairs, and the door opened.

Jackie's wide, clear eyes moved from me to Amber and back to me. We'd brought Hunch along, but I'd insisted he stay in the car for the moment.

"Can I help you?" Jackie asked, and in that second, I could picture her in the service industry as a cocktail waitress.

"Hi, yes. My name's Mallory Beck, and I'm working with the Honeysuckle Grove Police Department as a special consultant." You'd think after saying this enough, it would get less awkward, but every time, I still felt like a child playing dress-up. "And this is my niece, Amber. Can we please come in for a moment?"

Her eyes darted between us again. "Why? What's wrong?"

I tried to put on a disarming voice the way Alex was so good at doing. "We just have a few follow-up questions we hoped you could help with. I understand you were out of town at the time of Winston Blakely's passing?"

Her eyes moved side to side again, but this time, they didn't seem to focus on either of us. A second later, she burst out into a loud wail of a cry and covered her face.

I looked to Amber with a furrowed brow, but Amber kept her gaze steady on Jackie Reed.

After another couple of quieter cries and a few deep breaths, Jackie composed herself. "I'm so sorry. These antidepressants the doctor has me on are sending me into fits I can't seem to control."

"What kind of antidepressants are they?" I asked. I could get Alex to check with the medical examiner to confirm possible side effects if Google didn't answer my questions.

"I...um..." She left us for a moment to grab her purse out of a front closet. After digging inside, she pulled out a small pill bottle and flashed it in my direction. I already had my phone out, and without asking permission, I snapped a quick photo.

When I looked up, she seemed confused at my interest. I couldn't think of a good excuse as to why I'd be asking, but thankfully, Amber jumped in with her cherub-like innocence displayed on her face.

"My mom has been suffering since my dad died. I'm always on the lookout for something that will help her."

Jackie shook her head as she stuffed her pills back into her purse. "If I were you, I'd steer clear of this one. It has been nothing but drastic ups and downs for me. The doctor keeps changing my dosage, but I don't think it's helping." A new round of tears erupted, and she held up a finger for us to wait it out with her.

We did. I had to admit, if she was faking the emotions, she'd have to be a pretty talented actress.

When she pulled herself together again and wiped her tears away with a fresh tissue from a box on a small bureau in her entry, she said, "Now, you told me you had some questions? About Winston? Please, do come in." She pulled her door open wider, as if a minute ago she hadn't been reluctant.

I followed Amber inside, and she held out the casserole dish. "My aunt and I made you a Greek casserole." Amber didn't attempt the name. "I know how hard it can be to remember to eat and take care of yourself after something like this happens. My dad died only six months ago."

Jackie tilted her head, as though Amber's story had softened her. "I'm so sorry to hear about your dad. That's so sweet of you." She took the casserole but said, "I hope I'll be able to eat all of this by myself before Wednesday."

"Wednesday?" Amber and I asked at once.

"I have a flight booked to go back home. To Las Vegas," she added when we stared at her, waiting for more. She placed the casserole down on her bureau.

"This isn't your home?" I asked, looking around the entry. I didn't bother pulling off my boots. It didn't seem as though Jackie was going to invite us upstairs to sit down. "I noticed it's up for sale very quickly."

We waited through another short burst of tears. "I only planned to live here because of Winnie. We were going to open a mall together in Honeysuckle Grove."

"You and Winston? Together? What, exactly, was your part in these plans to open a mall?" I was certain my tone sounded condescending, but I didn't care. Perhaps her emotions were real, but her taking off with Winston's money two short weeks after his death was more than suspicious.

Jackie looked at her feet. "Well, I was the visionary. Winnie had never considered a shopping mall in this small town until we stopped by one time so I could meet his daughter. I suggested it seemed like Honeysuckle Grove was ripe for expansion with new housing being built each year, and a shopping mall might thrive here. The next thing I knew, he had bought a house for us."

"The visionary?" Amber asked before I could. It was the kind of thing people were always trying to get rich from, even if they hadn't done any actual work. My dad always tried to manipulate money out of people that way. "That's all the input you had?"

"Once we had it up and running, I was going to act as administrator." Jackie's eyes were wide and clear again. "Winnie had enough on his plate with Juniper Mills. Of course, he had to purchase and develop the land first, but we'd been looking at a couple of different locations that had promise."

I found her hot-and-cold emotional temperature changes unsettling, if not suspicious. They made her difficult to read. "And what kind of experience do you have that Winston would have hired you as an administrator for an entire shopping mall?" I asked.

She stared at me for a second. "Well, my parents' hotel, of course."

I raised my eyebrows in question, and soon she went on, realizing Amber and I had no clue what she was talking about. "My parents own the Mardi Gras Hotel in Las Vegas. I have managed the day-to-day administration for eight years. I've been training a new girl, but she hasn't been as quick as I'd hoped to catch on. I travel back there most weekends to ensure she's been on top of the daily hotel proceedings, as well as the casino, and of course, our luxury underground shopping mall."

"You were the administrator of all of those areas?" Disbelief was clear in Amber's tone, but Jackie didn't seem to notice.

"That's right."

"And that's where you were on the night of Winston's death?" I asked.

She shook her head and looked at her feet again. "I should have stayed. My flight wasn't booked until the next day, and I'd planned to attend the auction with him, but Cathy, our new hotel administrator, had really botched things, accepting far too many staff requests for New Year's Eve off. I headed straight for the airport as soon as I heard to see if I could get on standby."

"And what time did you eventually catch a flight?" I asked.

"They got me on a flight around eight. I was some kind of tired by the time I reached the hotel, and there was a crazy amount of mess to clean up from Cathy's mistake, but my night got infinitely worse when I got the call from Sheila on my cell phone."

"Sheila called you? That night?" I raised an eyebrow. "What did she say?"

Jackie pulled a phone from her back pocket. "I'll let you hear it. I don't know why, but as much as it upsets me, I haven't been able to bring myself to delete the message. It was the moment my whole life changed, all my plans with

Winnie...gone. Poof. And I was left with that nasty daughter of his saying awful things to me."

She navigated to her voicemail, and a moment later, Sheila's voice came through the speakerphone, filled with more venom in it than I'd ever have been able to imagine.

"I don't know where you're hiding out, tramp, but I know you did this to my dad. He never in a million years would have started up the generator in his office. I know that, and I'll prove you killed him if it's the last thing I do!"

Jackie clicked the message to save it again. Her emotions stayed in check as she said, "That was how I found out Winnie had died."

When Sheila and I discussed foul play at the funeral, she had acted as though it had been the first she'd thought of Jackie's involvement. I listened to the time stamp when Jackie resaved the message, and it was left at five in the morning on New Year's Day.

So definitely before Sheila and I had discussed the suggestion of foul play or Jackie being involved.

"I don't know why I even save that message." Jackie shook her head. "It only makes me feel worse every time I hear it."

"Why do you feel worse?" Amber asked.

Jackie let out a humorless laugh. "Would you like it if someone claimed you'd killed the person you loved more than anyone else in the world? And by his own daughter, no less?" She took a deep breath and pushed it out through pursed lips. "I should really just delete it."

"Wait!" I held out a hand. "I don't think it's in your best interest to keep listening to it, but you should have the police take a recording before you delete it. If there was any kind of foul play involved in Winston's death, it's important not to tamper with any evidence."

"Foul play? Evidence?" she asked with wide eyes.

I didn't have a good answer for why this might be evidence, as the last thing I wanted to do was get Jackie's mind on suspecting Sheila of harming her dad. Even if I was no longer certain that hadn't been the case, I was thankful when Amber changed the subject.

"We understand that Winston's entire estate was given to you?"

Jackie sighed. "Yes. Winnie named me as co-owner in a right of survivorship. It's been all I've been able to do to get that all wrapped up, as well as packing up the house before I leave Wednesday."

"All wrapped up?" I pushed.

Jackie nodded. "Winnie had very specific plans for what he wanted done with his possessions after his passing. It includes selling off stocks and bonds, but only at certain values. There were legal arrangements he wanted put in place to ensure his grandchild was raised the way he felt it ought to be. He had notes about a company that had interest in the outlet mall. I've been in touch with them and negotiating a price. That's why shortly after we met, he had his will re-drawn. He knew with my head for business, I could handle putting all of his wishes into place. If only I'd known it would come so soon, and I'd have a little over a week to do it."

"What sorts of specific things did he want done after selling off the stocks and bonds?" Amber asked. We were becoming a good tag team. When I was still processing information and taking notes, Amber often had the next question on the tip of her tongue.

"Well, he wasn't normally a big proponent of charity. He believed in people making their own way in the world and using the head God gave them to take care of themselves and their families. He had a great respect for the business school he attended right out of high school. It taught him many new ways of understanding finance that served him for the rest of his life. It's a small school in Michigan, and he wanted the bulk of his money to go to them, so they can build a new wing to allow for more students. I have to stay on top of it and ensure that actually happens, as businesses can be known to accept estate settlements and then not live up to their ends of the bargain."

"And where else was his money designated?" Amber asked. "Any to family or friends? Any money or assets allotted to you?"

Jackie nodded and headed up the stairs. She didn't invite us along, so I wasn't sure if I should be getting out of my boots or not. But a second later, she reappeared with a small statue of a lithe young woman. I wondered if it was supposed to be Jackie. It was abstract in the face and hair, so difficult to tell.

"We both fell in love with this antique baroque statue during the summer when we traveled to Paris."

If it was an antique, it clearly hadn't been modeled after her.

"He left the Lady in Waiting to me in his will. He knew it was special to me and would remind me of our trip together."

"And how much would you estimate the statue is worth?" I asked.

Jackie squinted down at it. "I think Winnie paid about four thousand for it, but he negotiated the price down. It was likely worth a thousand or two more." I stared at her with raised eyebrows, and she added, "Oh, but I would never sell it! Not in a million years."

"You both had an affinity for antiques?" I asked. "What did you think of the grandfather clock Winston bid on at the antique auction?"

She shook her head. "That, I'm afraid, is another thorn in my side. Winnie wanted that clock so badly, to have it set up in his home before the baby was born. I've gotten ahold of the winning bidder to see if there was any price he'd take for it, but I understand the clock was stolen on New Year's Eve. I'm not entirely sure what to do about that, or whether or not Winnie would even care about the clock now that he's gone, but I've asked Barry Rhodes to let me know if it's ever recovered and if he'd like to sell it at a profit."

"Barry Rhodes?" I asked.

"The winning bidder," she explained.

I made a note of the name.

"And so are you telling us that you have nothing to gain financially from Winston Blakely's death?" Amber was better at asking the bold and brutal questions. I couldn't stop myself from cringing. "Other than a statue worth less than ten thousand dollars."

She shook her head. "In fact, Winnie's insurance company has been giving me the runaround. It seems I might be out the cost of his burial until they've piled on all the red tape they can manage."

"You paid out of pocket for the burial? And the funeral?"

"I paid for the burial as soon as I got back into town, but Soron Sayward at Sayward's Funeral Home told me that Sheila Blakely had already been in to book and pay for the funeral herself. Apparently, she was planning to do it her way—no matter what her father wanted. I'd had Mr. Sayward perform a small burial-side service, just for me, but if I hadn't gotten it out of the funeral director, I wouldn't have even known the time and date of Sheila's so-called service."

"So you don't think the service at the funeral home would have been what Winston wanted?" I asked.

Jackie raised an eyebrow at me. "Would you have wanted your life celebrated with all of seven people there—one of which was only there as a special consultant for the police?" She motioned to me. Since she hadn't stayed for the reception, she didn't know that I'd actually been there as the caterer. But that didn't need correcting at the moment.

"And how would you have gathered more people to celebrate Winston's life?" Amber asked.

"I would have advertised it, of course!" She flapped her hands up. This was clearly a point that stirred up some emotion for her.

"Sheila Blakely said she advertised it both in Honeysuckle Grove and in Juniper Mills, where he used to live." I tilted my head and watched Jackie's reaction carefully.

She shook her head. "Have you looked into that? My guess is that either she posted something that wasn't at all inviting or she didn't announce it publicly at all. That child always seemed to want to keep her father to herself, and the poor man could never see what she really was."

"And what was she?" Amber and I both asked at once.

"A snake. Slithering around in the weeds and figuring out ways to get exactly what she wants, without working toward a single thing in her life. Winston's biggest regret was not bringing that girl up with a better head on her shoulders. I'll bet she was some surprised to find out her daddy didn't leave her a penny. She'll finally have to make her own way in this world."

"And what were Winston's stipulations about the raising of his grandchild, as stated in his will?" I asked, easily picturing the catfights that might ensue between Jackie and Sheila from this directive.

Jackie sighed. "I'll set up a trust in the grandchild's name after it's born. The money will be available for the child at eighteen for business school and living expenses, as long as the child keeps the family name. That's the gist of it."

I nodded and made a note. Amber and I thanked Jackie, and as we left, I could still hear her calling Sheila a snake in her own snake-like vicious tone.

Chapter Fifteen

I WAS INTERESTED TO look over Winston Blakely's will. If it had already been opened and read, it should have been filed with the county clerk's office by now. I wanted to check that Jackie's answers to our questions had been truthful, and once I confirmed that the bulk of Mr. Blakely's funds were allotted to a business school in Detroit, I felt as though I could clear Jackie of having a motive to kill Winston.

That all couldn't happen until Monday. For now, I had promised Alex I would stop by Chad's Antiques and ask a few questions about his auctioneer. But by the time we made it back to town, a wooden CLOSED sign hung in the window of Chad's Antique Village.

I sighed, slumping back into my seat as I decided where else to go.

Amber pointed down Main Street. "Sayward Funeral Home is right there. Why don't we see what Mr. Sayward thought of his interactions with Mr. Blakely's girlfriend and his daughter?"

"Good idea."

We found Soren Sayward outside the front door, just locking up for the night. "Mallory? Can I help you with anything?"

It was chilly outside, so I figured I'd better get right to the point. "The Blakely service was an interesting one, wasn't it?"

"Mmm. I understand Miss Blakely had expected a larger crowd." Soren's voice was as diplomatic as it had ever been.

"Did you know any of the attendees?" Amber asked.

He shook his head. "Only Miss Blakely. Oh, and Miss Reed," he added, almost as an afterthought.

"The lady in the leopard print?" When he nodded the affirmative, I went on. "How do you know her?"

He sighed. "Well, I suppose I don't, really, but she came by to make certain the proper arrangements for Winston were followed."

"And were they?" Amber asked.

Soren looked a little put off by being questioned by a teenager. He didn't know Amber, and so I put in my own question, hoping to settle his concerns. "I understand Mr. Blakely had only been living in town for six months and yet he had already filed his post mortem wishes with you?"

"Well, not with me," he explained. "Sayward Funeral Home is part of a larger online network. People can file from anywhere within the U.S., and when they pass, we simply look up what they'd planned for themselves."

"And what had Mr. Blakely planned?" I asked.

He shook his head. "He had not wanted to be cremated. He wanted the service advertised in Juniper Mills, which is where I understand he was from?" Before I could confirm that, Soren added, "But his daughter assured me she would take care of the advertising."

"And did she?" I watched him intently, but his ignorance over the subject was quickly obvious on his face.

"I'm afraid I couldn't say. When a loved one wants to take care of something themselves, it can be a path to healing." As he took in a breath and let it out in a sigh, I remembered back to making Cooper's funeral plans. Would taking some of it on myself have helped me along the path to healing? Soren interrupted my thoughts by adding, "I did find it odd that Sheila asked me not to post the service on our website."

"And Jackie Reed? Did she want anything strange?" Amber asked.

Soren shook his head. "Well. I suppose having a second private burial service was a little on the odd side, but she had been upset for not being a part of the funeral planning, so it made sense to me. I had the impression the two women were not on the friendliest of terms."

Amber and I nodded and looked at each other. For the moment, he had answered all of our questions, so we thanked him and left.

On the way back to my car, Amber said, "I think we should check in with Sheila Blakely to ask her a few more pointed questions."

I nodded my agreement. She didn't suggest calling first, and I often thought interviews worked out better if we took the interviewee by surprise, so I headed in the direction of Dylan and Sheila's townhouse without another word.

Amber stayed busy on her phone, doing what, I wasn't sure. It kept Hunch's attention rapt as he sat on her lap, staring at her screen.

Finally, when I was nearing Dylan and Sheila's street, Amber looked up and said, "Both Honeysuckle Grove and Juniper Mills have obituary listings. They mention the loving daughter he left behind and the grandchild Winston would not get to meet."

"Definitely sounds like Sheila wrote the listings. Her angry phone call to Jackie on New Year's definitely makes me think she's hiding something. Do you think she actually could be responsible for doing something to her own dad, though? It would have had to have been quite early on New Year's Eve, as I saw her around the community center many times throughout the auction." I shook my head. "I don't know. It's hard for me to wrap my head around her acting so distraught about losing her dad while she actually could be responsible for his death."

"Or..." Amber drew out the word. I glanced away from the road to try to see where her mind was going with this. "What if it was that boyfriend of hers who hurt her dad? He wasn't around much that night. Or what if Sheila's only playing the part of the perfect daughter in order to contest her dad's will and hopefully get some money out of it?"

I hadn't thought of that. "Well, at least she wasn't lying about posting to the papers."

"I don't know about that," Amber said as I pulled up in front of the townhouse where Sheila and her boyfriend lived. "Because there's no mention in either of these postings about a funeral service."

Before we left my Prius at the curb, I called Alex and left a voicemail about all we'd learned from Jackie's interview. "I'm tempted to believe her," I said before hanging up. "But just the same, we're going to double-check the will at the county clerk's office as well as the donation to the Michigan college from Winston's estate on Monday."

I turned to Amber after hanging up. "Am I missing anything, or are you ready to bombard Sheila Blakely with some questions?"

As we got out of the car and headed up the front walk toward the townhouse door, Amber said, "It feels weird to be interviewing someone without any food in our hands."

She was right, and so when the door opened and Dylan stood on the other side, the first thing that came to mind launched from my mouth. "Hi there. We wanted to make up a special meal for you and Sheila, but we wanted to check first that you didn't have any food allergies?" I tilted my head in the way that so many people had done with me after I'd lost Cooper, but in this case, I was only trying to look the part of compassionate bystander while I searched for the truth of the situation. "Is Sheila home, by the way?"

Dylan furrowed his brow and shook his head. He wore an oversized gray wool sweater that looked perfect for the weather. He had a few days' worth of stubble on his face, which was similar to when I'd seen him on New Year's Eve. I wondered if he always kept himself unshaven, and this made me wonder what he did for work.

"Do you know when she'll be home?" I pushed since he still hadn't said a word. I felt my countenance stiffening, as though preparing for him to slam the door in my face, and I wasn't sure why. Perhaps because he'd seemed to have so little compassion, he'd gone to bed when his very pregnant girlfriend went off alone to visit her recently deceased father.

"Green peppers," he said, and it took me a moment to realize he was finally answering my first question. "Not allergic, but they make Sheels sick something awful since the pregnancy."

"Okay, so no green peppers." I glanced at Amber, who had that driven look in her eyes.

"When did you say she was going to be home?" she asked.

Dylan shrugged. "I don't know. She's at her lawyer's. I have no idea how long those kinds of things take." He sounded annoyed, and I wasn't sure if it was about her going to the lawyer or about being ignorant about such things.

"What's she meeting with her lawyer about?" Amber asked. This was probably too pushy, but Dylan, surprisingly, didn't hesitate in answering.

"She's fighting about her dad's will." He shook his head. "She wants his money and thinks she deserves it more than the woman he'd been sleeping with."

"She wants to fight Jackie Reed through litigation for the money?" I confirmed. This, so far, lined up with everything Jackie had told us. I wondered if Sheila and Dylan were aware that Jackie was co-owner of his estate, and her story was that she wasn't keeping any of it. I wondered if they even knew she came from big Las Vegas money.

Dylan shook his head again. "I told her she shouldn't bother. Easy money brings easy problems. We're doing just fine on our own."

A voice called from within the townhouse. "You might need it for the wedding."

Dylan looked over his shoulder, and a second later, an older man appeared in the doorframe. He was the man with gray sideburns Amber had pegged as Dylan's father.

"Dylan's proposing tonight, right, son?" He clapped his boy on his back and then looked between me and Amber, some sort of revelation dawning on him. "Hey, you're that catering couple from New Year's Eve, right? Great spread, by the way." He rustled his son by the shoulder and backed into the townhouse again, but as he did, he said, "You should talk to these ladies about doing up a little food for your wedding."

Amber, ever the enthusiast about our catering pursuits, asked, "When's your wedding?" In a flash, she had her calendar app open on her phone, ready to book our next catering gig with or without my permission.

I was surprised when he told us, "Next weekend. Saturday afternoon."

Only a week away and he hadn't even proposed yet? I couldn't help my brow from furrowing. Plus, he planned to propose and get married right after her father had died? "Wow, that's soon," I told him. "You've been planning this a while, then?"

But Dylan said, "Nah, Dad just figured we should do it before the baby, or you know...born out of wedlock, confusion with names, and all that."

That seemed like an odd revelation in the midst of burying Sheila's father. But I supposed people didn't always think logically. I was surprised that Dylan didn't seem after Winston Blakely's fortune in the least.

I had to ask. "What do you do for work, Mr...?" I hadn't been told his last name.

"Thompson," he filled in for me. "But call me Dylan. I work at Hakim's alpaca farm, just outside of town."

"An alpaca farm?" I raised my eyebrows, wondering if his wool sweater could be made from alpaca wool. "What do you do there?"

This topic seemed to brighten Dylan's mood. "I pull an early morning shift, tending to Hakim's flock, but I'm also learning spinning and weaving. Everything's done right there on the farm." He held out his sweater. "Made this one myself."

I smiled. "It looks warm."

He nodded, eager to tell us more about what seemed like a job he was passionate about. "There are two types of alpaca fibers, and I've worked with the main one, Huacaya, for a long time. It's great for knitting scarves and sweaters and blankets, but I've just started working with Suri. It's much finer and has no lanolin, so it's hypoallergenic. You can even make suits with the stuff. Plus, it's water resistant."

"You should be a salesman for the stuff," Amber said with a chuckle.

He shrugged. "Well, yeah, I do that, too. It's worth a lot." He motioned over his shoulder inside. "Dad's opening a shop next month, about half an hour from here. You should check it out when it opens."

"We will," I said honestly. I'd prefer a more fitted sweater, but his was that kind of wool that made me want to reach out and touch it. I wondered what kind of price tag the sweaters went for, but I didn't get a chance to ask because Amber, always the better investigator of the two of us, launched in with another pertinent question.

"What kind of relationship did you have with Sheila's father?"

Dylan's natural-looking smile fell. "Winston? No one liked that old crab except Sheels and that girl of his, Jackie."

"So you didn't like the guy?" Amber pushed. "Did that dislike go both ways?"

Dylan sighed. "Yeah, probably. He was a cutthroat businessman. We just weren't made the same, you know? He put people out of business like he was ordering his morning coffee. I've been at my same job that I love for over ten years. I'm kind of surprised there wasn't a lineup of people waiting to spit on Blakely's grave."

"He's that disliked? Anyone in particular who had a beef with him?" I asked.

Dylan shrugged. "Couldn't tell you that, but go by his mall in Juniper Mills. I'd bet you'd find a lot of 'em ready to give you an earful about his merciless ways."

I'd make a note of this as soon as I got into the car, but for the moment, I hadn't introduced us as working with the police, and I'd rather keep it that way. "Sheila said something to me at the funeral—that she didn't think her dad would have been ignorant enough to plug in his generator and run it inside his office. What do you think?"

"I don't know about ignorant, but that man was self-preserving as all get-out. To tell the truth, I'm surprised the old man didn't live to be a hundred and fifty and out-live us all."

"So if someone had wanted to hurt the old man," I said, using his words, "who do you think it would have been?"

Dylan let out a humorless laugh. "Could have been a hundred people." He rubbed the sleeve of his wool sweater, looking down at it and pausing for a moment. I wondered if he was thinking or simply pausing for dramatic effect. "But if you ask me, Jackie Reed had more motive than anyone to off the old guy. At least, that's what Sheels thinks."

We thanked Dylan for his time and asked him to pass along a message to Sheila to call us about the wedding catering as soon as he had proposed, so we could get an idea of what she wanted for food.

Then we headed back to my place so we could meet Alex and go over all we had learned today.

Chapter Sixteen

AMBER AND I REHEATED our casserole dish of moussaka, as well as assembled a Greek salad with my own blend of dressing by the time Alex showed up.

He had barely made his way into the kitchen and taken his usual seat at my table before he blurted, "It looks like Sheila Blakely was right. There was foul play involved in her father's death."

"What?" Amber and I asked at once.

"Her father didn't die from carbon monoxide poisoning. The coroner says he's found internal proof of asphyxiation. We've officially upgraded the case to murder."

Strangely, I felt somewhat relieved at this revelation. As much as I did not want to think there had been another murder in Honeysuckle Grove, the wavering back and forth on whether there had truly been any foul play involved left my brain aimless and tired. Now, at least, I could focus.

"So do we know if the generator was turned on before or after he died?" Amber's quick mind didn't waste any time in catching up and rerouting to the new understanding of the case. "Were there any fingerprints on it?"

Alex shook his head. "No readable prints on the generator because of the snow, and only Winston Blakely's prints around the interior of his office. Clearly, if someone else entered his office, smothered him, and then set up a generator and turned it on, this person wore gloves."

"It's not a small machine," I put in. "I'm not sure I could have moved it into the office on my own."

Alex tilted his head back and forth. "It does have wheels. We didn't see where the wheel marks had come from, as the snow had covered those up before we arrived."

I had been trying to rule out Jackie and even Sheila, but apparently, I couldn't rule out anyone yet.

"Barry Rhodes has called three times today as well."

I recalled the name, but couldn't place it until Alex went on.

"He was the phone bidder who won the grandfather clock. As though I don't have enough to worry about right now, he's been putting pressure on us to find that clock, and unfortunately, he got Corbett on his side. If I worked twenty-four hours a day, I couldn't keep up with this caseload."

I felt bad for Alex and wondered if Jackie Reed's offer to buy the clock at a profit had instigated the extra pressure. His boss, Captain Corbett, often made arbitrary decisions that didn't seem to make sense. I suspected he took bribes. One day, when I didn't have so many other vital investigations to focus on, I wanted to use my newfound investigative skills to look a little closer at Captain Corbett. If only I could catch him in some sort of compromising position, it would be nice to finally have *him* scrambling to make things right, rather than Alex always trying to make up for the beef Corbett had with his dad.

"Any evidence to follow up on with the missing clock?" I asked. As inconsequential as it seemed next to a recent murder, if Alex had to do his best to solve it, I would put my best foot forward to help.

He nodded. "I finally got in touch with Ted Callaghan. Apparently, he had no desire for the grandfather clock. He said he'd always thought the thing was cursed, and he'd come to the auction out of morbid curiosity to see who the curse moved on to next. Ted said his dad had lost a lot of money over the years from pure bad luck, and that ticking clock in the background of all of their conversations had always felt like a bad omen."

"He couldn't have been lying?" Amber asked.

Alex shrugged. "That's always possible, but he invited me in to look around, and there was no sign of it anywhere in his house. Plus, he owned a smart car—much too small to move it."

"And did he have an alibi for after the auction?" Amber was sometimes like a dog with a bone over certain suspects, and I could feel her drive about Ted Callaghan.

"He went straight home. He said the neighborhood teenagers were setting off firecrackers in the street, so if necessary, I could go around and interview him. At this point, though, there are other things to focus on." He took in a breath and let it out slowly. "I've interviewed the driver of the cube van, Clive Wilson. He was run off the road by an old truck, but it was too dark to see the make or model, and he was knocked unconscious by the airbag in the cube van, so he didn't even get a look at the thieves."

"Hmm. Tire tracks? Paint residue?" I asked, thinking of the old truck I'd seen the auctioneer sitting in after the auction.

Alex shook his head. "Tire tracks were covered in snow by the time Steve arrived to investigate. We found some rust that didn't belong to the cube van, but other than that, there's not much to go on with paint residue."

"But the driver, Clive Wilson, definitely said the collision was deliberate?"

Alex nodded. "The truck came straight for him on a wide-open road. He laid on his horn in case the driver had fallen asleep, but the truck ran him straight into the ditch along the side of the road."

"And the only thing that was taken was that grandfather clock?" Amber confirmed.

Alex nodded. "We had Chad Wyatt go through the contents. He had a meticulous list of everything that either hadn't been bid on or would be claimed later—that was everything contained in the van. Not a single other item was missing, not even the antique jewelry that would have been simple to stuff in a pocket and sell later."

"So someone clearly had just come for the clock, the same clock Winston Blakely had been so desperate to win." I pulled the moussaka from the oven and put it directly on a hot mat on the table while it was still steaming. "Amber and I will look into the clock and see if we can find out what would make people so desperate to own it, especially since Ted Callaghan thought it was cursed. We tried to go by Chad's this afternoon to ask about the auctioneer, Roland, but we got there too late, and it was already closed. I remember him driving off in an old pickup truck right after the cube van left, though. We'll head back to Chad's first thing tomorrow and let you know what we find out about him."

Alex nodded, but his gaze stayed on my food as I delivered the Greek salad and pita bread to the table. I wondered if he'd remembered to eat today.

As we divvied up food and ate, we went over all of the details about the Winston Blakely case again. Alex kept forgetting small details, and Amber had to remind him. It made me wonder how many mistakes he might be making if he was overworked between the case Steve had him working on, the Winston Blakely case, and then the case of the missing clock that Corbett seemed to think was important enough for him to follow up on personally.

The black circles under his eyes were getting darker and darker each time I saw him. I wanted to say something about it, but at the same time, I had the feeling maybe there wasn't an easy solution to this particular problem. Perhaps me bringing it up would only cause more stress for Alex.

If Amber and I could lend a hand to help solve either of the cases, though, I decided right then that we would do everything we could to do exactly that.

Chapter Seventeen

SUNDAY MORNING, WHILE AMBER finished up her homework at the kitchen table, I headed over to Chad's Antique Village to ask a few questions about the missing grandfather clock.

Amber, of course, had wanted to come along, but I said I would need her company later to make a food delivery to Sheila and Dylan. She finally conceded and insisted I take Hunch along as my sidekick investigator.

As I got out of my Prius outside the antique shop, I was pleased to see the snow had been thawing, and now only a small layer of slush lay around my wheels at the curb. The slush, thankfully, was enough to deter Hunch from getting out on his own, and I snatched him up in my arms.

"Sorry, buddy. If you want to come along for this one, you're staying in my arms. We don't need any bull-in-china-shop moments. I definitely wouldn't be able to afford that."

In truth, Hunch was a careful cat and spent more time sniffing than he did touching anything he might consider a clue. But I still barely trusted myself to walk through Chad's precarious antique village without knocking anything over. I didn't need to be responsible for the two of us.

Both times when Amber and I had visited the local antique shop before, we'd had the place to ourselves. It surprised me when I opened the door and heard other voices, and on a Sunday morning no less. In fact, once I made my way through the open courtyard that led to Chad's main storehouse, I could make out at least three different voices.

I'd Googled to find out if Chad's Antique Village was open Sundays, and if so, what time it opened, as I planned to get here first thing. I was surprised to find out that others seemed to have the same idea.

"Eight hundred," a lady in her sixties said, holding an ornate wooden club in her hands.

Another couple stood nearby in the cramped shop. This couple was a little younger, and the man did all of the talking. "Eight-fifty."

In only a second, I realized the antique auction Chad held on New Year's Eve was not a one-time yearly event. Here, he didn't have an auctioneer, but it seemed his customers were more than willing to take on that part themselves.

"Nine hundred," a woman I hadn't noticed among the wares called out. She looked younger than me, and I wondered how she had nine hundred dollars lying around to spend on a piece of wood.

Chad stayed busy behind the counter, typing into his laptop and glancing up at everyone's offers.

The man huffed, raised both hands, and said, "We're out. It's not worth that."

This seemed to convince the sixtysomething woman as well. She nodded sadly at Chad, and he turned back to the young woman and said, "It's yours, Mrs. Humphrey, for nine hundred dollars."

Mrs. Humphrey strode forward, helped herself to the club from the older woman, and headed up to Chad's laptop with a credit card already outstretched. She didn't look as happy as I thought she should at winning. In fact, maybe she looked embarrassed, like she'd gotten caught up in the moment and now regretted paying too much.

The other bidders moved away from the counter and through the store to see if there was anything else they might want.

As soon as Chad finished processing Mrs. Humphrey's credit card, she turned and left, not noticing a single other item in the store. It made me think of how only the one clock had been stolen from the cube van. I supposed antique collectors knew exactly what they wanted and what they might be willing to do for it.

Chad finished typing into his laptop and then looked up. "What can I help you— Oh! Mallory! How nice to see you again. And may I say, the compliments I'm still hearing about your treats on New Year's Eve are too many to count."

I felt myself blush, but now Chad had his gaze on my cat. "He won't touch anything," I promised. "My cat is a bit of an investigator. He just likes to sniff around for clues."

Chad let out a humorless chuckle. "Well, maybe your cat can figure out who stole the grandfather clock from the auction. I've got the bidder and the bank both breathing down my neck."

"The bank, too?" I asked.

"As a repossession, the starting bid was set low, at what they absolutely needed for it, even though it was worth at least thirty thousand."

"Thirty thousand dollars for a clock?" I asked.

Chad nodded. This was old news to him, and not a very impressive price where antiques were concerned, it seemed. "The bank is insisting because it was in my possession, it should fall under my store's insurance. The winning bidder is saying the same thing, but my insurance company is giving me the runaround about covering it. I normally don't carry those big-ticket items. If I'm sued for it, they'll put me out of business."

I could well imagine with the number of antiques Chad collected, he had been in business here for many decades.

"Tell me about the winning bidder," I said. "Has he been in to see you since the clock went missing?"

Chad shook his head. "He's not one of my regular clients, either." He scrolled through his laptop. "His name was Barry Rhodes, but I'm afraid that's all I know about the man. Part of me wonders if he stole the clock himself, so he could end up with both the clock and the money."

Chad wasn't too shabby when it came to smart investigative ideas. This hadn't occurred to me, but it did now. I'd have to run that suggestion by Alex to see what he thought.

"What about your auctioneer, Roland... something-or-other?"

"Roland Conway," he put in. "What about him?"

"How much do you know about the man? I saw him drive off right after the cube van left." Normally, I wouldn't give this much information, but I didn't get the feeling Chad and Roland had much beyond a civil working relationship, and I wanted Chad to think this over carefully.

Chad shook his head and looked down at the counter in front of him. "He may have left at the same time, but I can't imagine..." He shook his head again. "I mean, he had to get home to his daughter, so..."

When Chad trailed off and didn't say anything else, I figured I'd have to dig more to get him talking. "His daughter? How old is she?"

"Around twelve, I'd say," Chad told me. "He mentioned more than once that he didn't like leaving her alone on New Year's Eve. I think it was his way of pushing me to offer him a little extra money. In truth, I'd planned to go around and offer everyone a little bonus for the evening, as it had seemed to go so well, but now with the missing clock and the insurance problem, I may need every penny I've got."

I was tempted to turn around and give my pay back. Poor Chad looked awfully stressed. But I knew how Amber would react to that.

"Do you think Roland would be capable of stealing that clock—since he seemed to need the money?"

Chad laughed at that. "Roland? No, not a chance. How would he move the thing all on his own? Plus, he'd never be able to sell it without plenty of people knowing about it. Roland knows antiques well enough to know that selling an important piece like that clock comes with a trail. Whoever took it wanted to keep it. That's one thing I'm quite certain of."

I wasn't as convinced. There was always the possibility that the auctioneer had connections in the antique world and could have found a private buyer. I put Hunch down for a second, instructed him to "Stay!" and made a few notes on my notepad. "Do you have a phone number or address for Mr. Conway?"

He found a phone number on his computer and read it off to me. "Are you working with the police again?"

I nodded. "Helping, yes." At least I hoped I was. Hunch was already sniffing around at the lamps and ornaments within his reach. He wasn't giving any one thing much attention and didn't get too close. I added a note about Barry Rhodes, so I'd remember to talk to Alex about him later. "So this Mr. Rhodes has never been into your store?"

Chad shook his head. "I don't think so. At least he's never purchased anything, or I'd have him in my records."

I remembered from our last case that Chad kept meticulous records of his customers and the pieces they had purchased. "What can you tell me about the grandfather clock? Did you know much about it before the bank brought it to you?" Part of me also wondered if someone at the bank could be trying to double-cross Chad to get both the money and the clock.

Chad nodded and didn't need his laptop for these details. "It was late nineteenth century. The clock was nicknamed 'Only' because of the Arabic inscription under the swinging pendulum. The inscription is interesting. It's about the seriousness of loyalty to one's family. It is highly regarded, as grandfather clocks go. A real prize piece."

"That's its nickname? Could I find out more about it by looking that up online?" I suspected I'd get a lot of irrelevant results if I simply looked up "Only" and "Grandfather clock."

But Chad typed into his laptop again and then turned it toward me, making my heart skip a beat that the move might knock one of his precious wares to the floor. But he seemed in control of his little shop, and nothing fell. "Here's a Wikipedia page on it." He pointed to a long complicated word in a language made up of squiggly characters that looked nothing like English. "This is the official name of it."

I pulled out my phone and asked him if he'd mind if I took a snapshot of his screen. He didn't mind.

"Maybe your cat does know something about investigative work," he said as I concentrated on getting a clear shot. "That there is another Zanğabīl piece, although not worth nearly as much as the Only clock."

I looked over at where Hunch sniffed around the spindly legs of a small table made from reddish wood. "Are all of those... Zang-ga-beel—" I raced on with my words, as I knew I'd butchered the pronunciation. "Are they all that reddish-brown?"

Chad nodded. "I believe the word means ginger. They're not common around the U.S., so whenever I see one, I try to get my hands on it. That's why the second the bank sent me the list of antique contents from their recent foreclosure, I immediately spoke up for the grandfather clock for my big auction." He looked down and shook his head. "Now I wish I hadn't."

I couldn't seem to stop my optimism from poking out its head and trying to make him feel better. "I'm going to do everything I can to find that clock, Chad. Don't you worry."

But I worried a lot as I scooped up my cat and left.

Because if Roland wasn't a serious suspect, and if the grandfather clock's resale would have left an obvious trail, did I even have anything to go on?

Chapter Eighteen

LATER THAT MORNING, I split my time between making chicken parmesan for Dylan and Sheila and researching the grandfather clock on my laptop at the edge of my kitchen counter. Amber was deep into her biology homework at the table—a subject she hated, but she worked hard at it because Alex suggested it might one day help her with investigative work.

She sat back in her chair and sighed, which was my cue to give her a break from her studies.

"This is interesting," I said. She stood and came over to look at the screen of my laptop. "The reason these clocks are worth so much is because there were only ever three of them made."

"Still, three seems like a lot for a clock that's nicknamed Only." Amber laughed at her own joke, but there was some truth to that.

"All the Zanğabīl pieces were produced by one family over three generations," I read from the Wikipedia page. "This particular brand of antique died out with them. There's a paragraph-long inscription on all three, which loosely translates that a person should not divide their loyalty and that loyalty to family is paramount."

"Can you find out where the other two clocks are?" Amber asked.

I flipped to another tab in my browser to where I had a website open for a museum in France. "One of them is here. I'm not sure how to track down antiques if they're privately owned, though, but Chad made it sound as though that was easily done. Maybe that's another question for him."

"Maybe," Amber agreed. "But if we keep bugging the guy, we'll have to at least bring him some more baking. Did you call Roland Conway yet?"

I shook my head. In truth, I'd been putting it off. He wasn't the most pleasant of men. But now that she'd brought it up, I picked up my phone and dialed the number from my notes.

He picked up on the first ring, sounding out of breath or like he was in a hurry. "Hello?"

"Hi, Mr. Conway?" My voice came out too bright, as if I was already trying to compensate for his grumpiness. "This is Mallory Beck. I met you at the antique auction on New Year's Eve?" When he still didn't respond, I added, "I was the caterer?"

"What's this about?" he grumbled, in way of an answer. "I'm busy."

I felt as though it would take more work to get his address out of him willingly than it would to get right to the point of why I was calling. I wouldn't be able to gauge his reactions to my questions by looks, but at least I had him on speakerphone, so Amber could help me judge them by sound. "Right. Well, I'm working as a special consultant with the local police department. Were you aware there was a theft that night?"

"A theft at one of Chad's auctions? Now that's a first." He sounded genuinely surprised. "I bet Sara must be pretty shaken up. Maybe I should call her."

"Sara?" Amber and I looked at each other in confusion.

"Chad's administrator. She would have had the money all night. You're saying she was robbed by someone, right?" Roland let out a humorless laugh. "If I catch the guy who did that to her..."

I was surprised both by his jumping to the wrong conclusion and for his protectiveness over this Sara person. I wondered if she was the lady with the laptop on the stage that evening.

"Actually, this theft had nothing to do with Sara," I explained.

"Oh. So she had already given the cashbox to Chad? Well, that's a relief. He can afford it." There was the man with the chip on his shoulder I'd met on New Year's Eve.

"Actually, it was an item that was stolen. You haven't heard anything about that?" I asked.

"Can't say I have. And why are you calling me, exactly?" Reading voices was much more difficult than reading faces, but I sensed a strong defensiveness in his.

"I'm sure you'll remember the antique grandfather clock that sold for over twenty-five thousand dollars that night."

A pause followed. "No, that couldn't have been. I saw the security guard pack it up with my own eyes. It couldn't have been stolen. You must have your facts wrong." He certainly sounded as though his ignorance over the subject was truthful.

"I'm afraid the cube van that was delivering the clock to a secure location was run off the road that night. Nothing else was taken," I added.

This pause was longer. "Okay, but I still don't get why you're calling me about this. The last time I saw the clock, it was being loaded into the van."

"And you drove away right after the van did," Amber put in. She had been sitting by silently, letting me conduct the interview, but it seemed she could no longer hold herself back.

"I went straight home!" he practically yelled. "My daughter, Julie, was on her own. She's barely eleven. I had to get home to her. Are you accusing me of something here, or what?"

"Not at the moment, no, we're not," I told him. "But is there anyone who can confirm what time you arrived home that night?"

"Julie can." As if he knew this wouldn't be enough, he went on explaining himself. "I knocked on Ellie Harper's door when I got in. She lives in the apartment beside us, and she was willing to be around as a nearby adult for Julie, just in case of emergency. Whenever I get in late, I give a couple of quick knocks to let her know I'm home again. She likes it that way." The guy's words rattled out so quickly, he was working himself into a tizzy.

"If you could get me her phone number, as well as a number for Chad's assistant, Sara, that would be really helpful," I said in my calmest voice, hoping he would calm down, too.

I heard him taking a couple of breaths on the other end, but then he slowly listed off Ellie's and Sara's phone numbers. "Do you want to talk to Julie?" he asked.

"That won't be necessary for now," I told him. "What do you know about selling antiques? Is this a regular gig for you? Do you own any yourself?"

I could sense him shaking his head on the other end even before he spoke. "I've got no use for them. I used to work as a voice actor, narrating audiobooks mostly, but when work dried up, a friend suggested I might be good at auctioneering. I tried it and had a natural knack. End of story. I really don't know anything about antiques and can't believe what people will spend on them."

He wasn't alone there. I looked at Amber, who nodded in agreement that we were done here for the moment. Then I thanked him, said goodbye, and phoned Ellie Harper right away before he had a chance to talk with her.

She corroborated his story, but of course, she hadn't seen his face that night. It could have easily been his daughter knocking on the neighbor's door.

But for the moment, I was inclined to believe him.

After that, Amber got back to her biology homework, and I pulled the chicken parmesan out of the oven. I left the heat on, as I figured Amber might be right. No matter who else we decided to talk to today, it couldn't hurt to have some baking power on our side to help us along in our interviews.

An hour later, Amber had finished her biology homework, and I had finished making two chicken parmesans—one for Sheila and her boyfriend and one for us—as well as enough apple and cinnamon scones to feed all of our interview subjects and suspects combined.

Amber ate at the counter while she packed up a special to-go container for Alex. "I don't think he's been taking care of himself. Can we drop this by the station for him on our way to Sheila's?"

It wasn't on the way. In fact, it was in the opposite direction, but I wasn't one to argue if we had any reason at all to drop by and see Alex. Besides, Amber was right, and we had to make sure he took care of himself.

I felt bad that I didn't have much helpful news to share on the investigation front, but I hoped he might be able to get us an address for Barry Rhodes so we could drop by and take care of that interview this afternoon. There were many reasons to suspect any serious antique collector who might have wanted the prized grandfather clock for themselves, but you never knew what other details you could find out during an interview.

We arrived at the police station just after two, but unfortunately, Alex wasn't there.

"He's at the bank this afternoon with Steve," the police receptionist, Samantha, told me.

Amber and I had been working with Alex for so long that she knew me well enough to share this sort of thing. Alex must have had the same thought Chad did—that perhaps someone was trying to get both the clock and the insurance money for themselves. I was glad to hear that Steve Reinhart was helping with the missing clock case, and it hadn't all been lumped onto Alex, but it still seemed nonsensical that Corbett had them so focused on that case when they had just discovered Winston Blakely had been murdered.

Unless, of course, the missing clock had something to do with his murder.

"Can I leave this for him?" Amber asked, holding up the mini-casserole dish of chicken parm and the side Tupperware container of scones. She'd given him enough for both lunch and dinner, in the event that he didn't have time to join us later.

Samantha nodded and accepted the food. "Smells good."

Amber would never offer up any of Alex's food, but I couldn't seem to help myself. "There are lots of scones in there, if you'd like one."

Samantha smiled and nodded, but didn't open the container. She could probably feel Amber's protective glare.

Before we left, I scrawled a quick note to go with the food. In it, I gave the name of the brand of the antique clock, as well as its nickname. I didn't know if it would help Alex at all, but if Corbett was making him focus on this case, at least Alex would have something to show his boss if he hadn't come up with anything new on his own.

From there, I drove across town to Sheila Blakely's townhouse. Again, we hadn't given any warning, but with the casserole in tow, plus the question of whether or not Amber and I would cater Sheila and Dylan's wedding, we felt like we had ample reason to drop in unannounced.

But it was Dylan who answered the door a second time. His clothes and hair looked disheveled, and if not for the smell of barnyard wafting off him, I might have thought he had still been sleeping at this late hour in the afternoon. But then I recalled his job at the alpaca farm started early.

"Off work already?" Amber asked the question I had been thinking.

Dylan nodded. "For now. I start at four, usually take a couple hours off in the afternoon. Most days I go back in the later afternoon to spin the wool or weave a blanket or a sweater."

"Wow, that's a lot of overtime," Amber observed. We hadn't actually gotten an alibi out of anybody besides those we saw at the auction for the night of New Year's Eve, but now that the death had been officially upgraded to murder, I supposed I should swing the questions in that direction.

But Dylan said, "Not overtime, no. I go in on my own. The owner, Mr. Hakim, said if I took the early morning shift, I could pay ten cents on the dollar for my own wool if I spin it. There's really good money in alpaca wool products, and with a baby on the way, plus a wedding, I'm working hard every hour I can to save for our future."

It made me feel bad for jumping to conclusions about his callous attitude for leaving Sheila on her own on New Year's Eve, especially since he hadn't known anything was really wrong at the time. I also felt bad for keeping him here when he probably should be resting.

But not bad enough that I'd cut my questions short and leave.

"Is that where you were on New Year's Eve? Is that why you only made it to the auction for a short time?"

Dylan sighed. "I probably wouldn't have come at all if Sheila hadn't wanted me to. She thought her dad might buy her something nice if she spent the evening with him at the thing, and she was always trying to prove how much he loved her. To me or to herself, I wasn't always sure."

"You don't care for antiques?" I pressed.

He scowled. "No, I don't have any interest in expensive trinkets." I wondered if we could rule him out of taking the grandfather clock if that was the case. "I told Sheila she should stay home and rest, but she wouldn't listen. Next thing I knew, she was bidding on a clock for her old man—one we definitely couldn't afford. But Sheels sometimes has a mind of her own. I just couldn't stay and watch."

"So where did you go from the community center that night?" I pushed.

Dylan looked up, as if he was trying to remember. "I took my dad to the farm to show him a bunch of what I'd made. Then he dropped me off at my car at the auction. I came in to say good night to Sheels and then went home to sleep for the night."

"And what time was this?" I asked.

Dylan shrugged. "Probably close to midnight. I had to get up again at four the next day."

"Is there anyone else who could account for you arriving home at that time?" Amber asked, catching onto my line of questioning. She still held the casserole in front of her. She was often hesitant to offer food to someone until we needed to soften them for more answers or until she was convinced they weren't guilty of murder.

Dylan started to shake his head, but then snapped his fingers. "Well, sure. Bart and Bella next door. They were having some big New Year's blowout. Hadn't bothered to invite me and Sheels, but thought it was their right to blast their music through the neighborhood. Bella was out on her porch vaping with some girlfriends when I got home. I told her I had to get some sleep, and they'd better turn their music down, or I'd call the cops."

I glanced over to the townhouse he motioned to. "And did they turn it down?"

Dylan shrugged. "A little. I was in a lousy mood after Sheels wouldn't listen to me about bidding on the clock. I didn't want to argue anymore. I just wanted to put in my earplugs, cover my head in a blanket, and get a few hours of sleep before I had to wake up again."

Amber held out the casserole. "We brought a chicken parmesan for you and Sheila." Amber ducked her head side to side, as if trying to see past Dylan's broad shoulders into the townhouse. "Is she home, by the way?"

We already knew Sheila's whereabouts the night of her father's murder, but it might prove interesting to interview the two together.

But Dylan shook his head. "Nah, she's at work until five."

"She's still working? What does she do?" Between the two of them, they definitely seemed to be working hard to provide a good life for their baby.

"She's a clerk at a clothing store. Her dad got her the job, and I think she was trying to prove something to him by working right up until the day she gave birth. I'm hoping now she'll actually consider maternity leave. Her feet are killing her by the time she gets home each day."

"Each day? Does that mean she's full-time?" Amber asked.

Dylan nodded. "She gets Fridays and Saturdays off, and Sundays are a little shorter of a day." He looked off into the distance. "And at least Juniper Mills has a bigger hospital if she goes into labor while she's at work."

"Wait, she works all the way at the Juniper Mills outlet mall?" I asked.

Dylan sighed. "Yup. Like I said, it was about proving something to her dad. I suppose it'll take some time for the realization to sink in that she doesn't have to do that anymore."

I checked my watch. It was already three thirty. We could wait and track her down tomorrow, but I liked the idea of questioning her about her voicemail to Jackie Reed at the end of a long day.

After all, we had to get to the truth of what really happened to her father.

Chapter Nineteen

IT WASN'T DIFFICULT TO spot Sheila Blakely through the front window of Bella's Boutique, right near the food court in the Juniper Mills outlet mall. She wore a fashionable emerald sweaterdress, and her belly led the way around the store as she tidied up in time for closing.

"Should we interrupt her?" Amber asked, always the eager one.

I raised my eyebrows at her. "It's fifteen minutes. I think we can wait."

I was about to sit on a nearby bench, but Amber's gaze darted in all directions. "We should stop in at some other stores. See if people knew Winston Blakely and what they thought of him."

It wasn't a bad idea, although I felt like we already had enough people who disliked the man. Without waiting for my approval or direction, Amber marched across the outdoor aisle and straight into a discount supplement store, which appeared empty other than one clerk.

I followed her at a distance. We hadn't come up with a plan of whether we should be related to each other or with the police.

By the time I got into the store, Amber seemed to already be on her second question. "So you never actually met the guy in person?"

The clerk was a young woman in her early twenties. Her store-issued red T-shirt stretched taut over muscular arms.

"Nah, but everyone here knows the guy by reputation. He's shut down more than one store just like that." She snapped her fingers and looked between the two of us, intuitive enough to understand that we were together. "You're wondering about Blakely, too? Yeah, I was told on the day I was hired that if someone named Blakely came into the store, call the manager right away. He put his number on speed dial into all of our phones."

"Because your boss was afraid Mr. Blakely might shut him down?" I asked.

The girl shrugged. Her name tag read RASHANDA. "I guess. He'd done it with at least three stores, or so I've heard."

"Do you think he did it without reason? Or do you think the stores he shut down weren't paying their rent or something?" Amber asked.

"Even still, don't you give people some notice?"

"Did you know that Winston Blakely's daughter works just across the way there?" I asked, searching her face for recognition.

Rashanda's brow furrowed, and she immediately started tidying up protein bars and energy shots from beside the till.

"I don't think she's about to close anybody down." I adopted a calming voice. "I was just wondering if you knew her."

Rashanda shook her head, but her gaze repeatedly darted out the front window.

"Did you know any employees of the businesses that were shut down here?" Amber asked. She was always on top of the smart questions.

The girl shook her head. "Mr. Rob told me about a couple of them, though. There was a shoe store." She pointed down the aisle in the opposite direction of Bella's Boutique. "And my favorite sportswear store closed at least six months ago. I don't know if that one was because Blakely kicked them out, but it could have been."

We asked what these two stores were called, and I made a note of them in my notebook. When I looked up again, Rashanda's gaze was on her front window, and out of instinct, I followed it. All of the five people within my vision were headed toward the mall exit, but I stopped still when familiarity struck.

"Who's that man?" I asked and pointed at a man in a suit with graying hair. He wore a name tag, which I could only see the shape of on his suit jacket. He was the same man who had been seated in front of me at Winston Blakely's funeral, the one who hadn't come downstairs to join in on the reception.

Rashanda shrugged. "I don't know his name, but he manages the sushi shop around the corner. I've heard rumors that it's on its last legs, too. Not surprising, really. It's a high-end place, and most shoppers are here to save money, right?"

All I offered was a nod for an answer. Then Amber and I thanked her and headed for the door, hoping we could catch up with the sushi manager.

Chapter Twenty

AMBER AND I CAUGHT up with the suited man just as he reached for a door handle to get into his black Volvo.

"Excuse me, sir?" Amber called.

He stopped and turned back, but then looked behind him as though Amber might be calling someone else.

"We just had a few questions, if you wouldn't mind," I put in, wondering if an adult voice in the mix would help him clue in that we were serious.

He shook his head roughly and pulled open his car door. "I'm in a hurry."

"Actually, sir." Amber quick-stepped toward him and placed a hand on his open car door before he could get in. We were on the bottom floor of a three-story open-air parking garage, and her voice echoed when she said, "We're special consultants with the Honeysuckle Grove Police Department, and I'm afraid these questions are of an official nature."

My mouth went dry, as it always did when Amber boldly introduced us this way. The man looked from my teenage sidekick to me for confirmation. Thankfully, we'd left my cat at home for the drive to Juniper Mills. I forced a swallow and squeaked out the words, "That's right."

"What kind of police business? What do you need from me?" In an instant, his voice had smoothed out to an even, almost helpful tone.

"You were at the funeral of Winston Blakely," I offered as a statement, rather than a question. "Can you tell me how well you knew the man?"

He took in a deep breath and let it out in a sigh. "Not terribly well. I've had a restaurant here for the last couple of years, so of course, we've had interactions."

"Interactions?" Amber jumped on this.

"Day-to-day stuff. Lease payments, holiday hour changes, that sort of thing."

"Can I get your name?" I asked. "And the name of your restaurant."

The man didn't hesitate. "I'm Percy. Mahoney. I own Dragon Sushi, just past the main food court on the right."

He certainly seemed helpful enough. I asked my next question as I continued making notes. "We've heard rumors that your restaurant is on its way out of this mall. Is there any truth to that?"

The man sighed again. "I've been looking for a new location, yes, as well as trying to get out of my lease a little early, but Winston wouldn't have it, so I'm stuck here until the end of summer. My restaurant really doesn't cater to this mall's clientele," he explained.

That lined up with what Rashanda from the supplement store had said, but Amber jumped on this with what sounded very close to an accusation. "So having Winston Blakely out of the way probably makes it easier to get out of your lease early, right?"

"I wouldn't say so, no." His voice remained calm. "The new owners haven't even made the sale public yet. I understand they're still waiting for everything to calm down with the will so the sale can go through. None of us have even met them yet, so I would expect they'll want to keep the machine of this mall running as smoothly as possible until they have time to start considering individual stores. I can't imagine that happening before summer."

"How did you feel about Mr. Blakely?" I asked, trying a different tactic. It didn't sound as though he held a lot of hatred toward the man. "And if you didn't know him well, why attend his funeral?"

Percy Mahoney closed his car door, seemingly ready to give us as much time as we needed. "I can't say Blakely and I always saw eye to eye, but I had great respect for him as a business-man. In fact, even though he wouldn't let me out of my lease early, he'd given me tips of more than one location outside of the mall that I might want to secure for myself. Properties he'd considered purchasing himself. I haven't found anything quite suitable yet, but I appreciated the help."

"So you were at the funeral to pay your respects?"

Amber barely gave him a chance to answer my question before she barreled on with her own. "Can you tell us where you were the night of New Year's Eve?"

He furrowed his brow at her, I suspected just now realiz-ing he was actually being interrogated for something serious. "Well, sure. I was at the Radisson, catering a party they were holding in their lounge. They don't have a restaurant onsite, so they brought us in as part of the celebration."

I'd driven by the Radisson in Juniper Mills, but had never been inside. Still, it seemed like an easy enough alibi to check out.

As if Percy Mahoney could read my mind, he added, "Go ask my staff. Two of them are still closing up, and my whole crew was at the Radisson that night. We kind of treated it like our own staff party and ended up having a great time."

Amber launched into three questions in a row on how often he caters events and how he finds new gigs—definitely not noteworthy on this case—but I checked my phone, and it was already two minutes after five.

"We have to go!" I told them both. "Thank you, Mr. Ma-honey. You've been a great help, and we'll be in touch if we have any more questions."

Amber looked annoyed, but she didn't fight me as I tugged her back toward the mall, so we wouldn't miss our opportunity with Sheila Blakely.

Chapter Twenty-one

WHEN AMBER ELBOWED ME, I looked up to see Sheila Blakely leaving through the front door of Bella's Boutique.

Sheila did a double take when she saw me. "Mallory? Is everything okay?"

"Oh, yes, yes." I pasted on a bright smile. "We dropped a casserole off to Dylan today. He mentioned you worked here, and Amber and I got a hankering to do a little shopping." I motioned between the two of us, and Amber wore the cherub-like innocent look that seemed as easy for her to slip on as a spare purse.

This immediately disarmed Sheila. "Well, I'm just off work, and I'm afraid the mall is closing."

"No worries." I waved a casual hand. "We got what we came for." Before Sheila could notice we had no bags, I went on. "Hey, while I have you here, I just need to ask you a couple of questions regarding your dad." I motioned to the bench I'd been about to sit on earlier, but Sheila's eyes darted in every direction.

"Here?" she asked.

"I promise it won't take long." The Juniper Mills outlet mall was an open-air mall. While the stores would all be closing, we would be in no rush to leave the aisles or benches, even if it was a bit chilly.

Thankfully, either exhaustion or our authority won out because Sheila lowered carefully onto the bench around her belly.

"Are you planning to work right up until your due date?" Amber asked. We already knew the answer to this, but it was the kind of disarming question Amber was great at.

Sheila nodded. "Dylan wants me to take mat leave early, but I'm learning so much here, and after the baby comes, I plan to get in the works of opening my own store in Honeysuckle Grove."

"With a newborn baby?" I asked, my eyebrows spiking up on their own.

"Well, sure. I mean, I'll need a few weeks to recover..."

A few weeks? Even though I'd never had a chance to have my own babies, my sister, Leslie, had demonstrated how all-consuming they could be. Leslie had finally gotten back to work last year when her kids were all into their double digits.

I couldn't seem to help myself from driving this point home. "Oh, is Dylan going to stay home and help with the baby, then?"

I knew the answer before she shook her head. "We'll figure it out."

Would they? Or was she just delusional? "I understand your dad's will didn't contain everything you expected?"

Sheila leaned sideways on the bench and rubbed her lower back. "That tramp of his must have really done a number on him to make him change his will and leave her everything. Doesn't matter. I've already talked to my lawyer, and she assures me we can fight it."

I wondered what grounds Sheila's lawyer figured she could fight on. Or perhaps Sheila was only believing what she wanted to believe again.

"So you think Jackie Reed convinced your father to change his will and then plugged in his generator inside his office to kill him?" Amber was great at disarming questions, but she was also fantastic at these on-the-nose kind.

Sheila opened her eyes with forced innocence. "Well, that's what Mallory suggested."

I squinted, willing to push past her half-truths. "I understand you phoned Miss Reed and left a voicemail accusing her
of as much on the very night your dad died."

Her eyes snapped to me. "Who told you that?"

"I had a conversation with Miss Reed." I perched on the
edge of the bench across from Sheila, but she was starting to
look so uncomfortable both by her back and this conversation
that I was tempted to stand back up so she could stretch
out. Amber stayed looming above, keeping the "authority that
comes with stature," as she called it.

Finally, Sheila sighed and put her face in her hands above
her big belly. "I was so emotional that night, and I needed
somebody to blame. I couldn't help myself." Her voice sounded as though she was crying, but when she pulled her hands
away, her eyes were dry. "I was so upset, and it didn't seem
like it could be real. I lashed out, and I'd say I was sorry about
it, but if she truly killed my dad for his money, I'm definitely
not sorry."

Her excuse seemed weak, at best. "You said you placed
notices of your dad's funeral in the Honeysuckle Grove and
Juniper Mills newspapers, but we couldn't find anything of the
sort."

"I—I sent obituaries mentioning his death." She looked at
her lap, not meeting my eyes. "I figured anyone motivated to
find out about his service would find a way."

"Why would you want to keep it quiet?" Amber asked.

I piggybacked on her question with my own. "And why tell
us to prepare food for fifty?"

Tears finally started to form at the corners of Sheila's eyes.
"Look, if your dad had a lot of enemies, would you want
them showing up for your last chance to honor him and say
goodbye?" She wiped her eyes. "I loved my dad. I wanted to
keep that time to myself, and I didn't want to send an open
invitation to anyone who might want to spit on his grave."

Her emotion seemed real. Whether or not her excuses made sense, I was quite sure they made sense to her. Especially when she went on.

"Word could have gotten around. It could have still been a busy funeral, and I had no idea what to expect. To be honest, it seemed like my dad became yesterday's news the day after his death." She dabbed her eyes again.

I got back to the topic of Jackie. "What if I told you Jackie Reed couldn't have killed your dad and she didn't keep his money for herself, either?"

Sheila shook her head slowly. "That's not true. It can't be."

I didn't know for sure yet, of course. But I had a sneaking suspicion that Alex would come back with the time of death and it would put Jackie Reed in the clear. I also suspected that the allocation of Winston's money would check out.

"Let's just say for a second that it is true," I said. "And let's say someone else wanted to kill your dad." Sheila would hear soon from the police that this case had been officially upgraded to a murder investigation, but I didn't want to blab anything I shouldn't. "Who else do you think it could have been?"

Sheila looked down the aisle between shops, lost in thought for several seconds. "I suppose it could have been a lot of people. Dad made people angry, but angry enough to kill?"

"Anyone around here that he had put out of business?"

Sheila scanned the various stores within eyesight. "Sure, I guess." She didn't sound convinced. "There was Jim McNaulty, who owned the frozen yogurt shop in the food court."

She listed another couple of names and stores. I listened carefully for her to corroborate the two stores the girl in the supplement store had told us about, and finally, she did with one of them. But I could no longer concentrate on the name of the shoe store after she mentioned its owner.

"Dad shut down Leather Bound over a year ago, but I can't imagine its owner killing Dad. I mean, he showed up at his funeral."

"He did?" Amber and I both asked at once.

Sheila looked between us. "Sure. The sushi guy was there, too. I don't keep track of their names."

"Are you talking about Percy Mahoney?" I asked, watching her for recognition.

She nodded slowly. "That sounds right."

"And what about the owner of Leather Bound? You don't have any idea of his name?" I had my notepad out and ready.

She shook her head. "Terry or Barry something-or-other?" She asked it as a question, and Amber immediately answered it with her own question.

"Barry Rhodes?" she asked.

"Yes, I think that's it," Sheila said. "Poor guy. He must be suffering after Dad shut down his business. Did you notice his disheveled suit?"

I had. Which left Amber and me with one big question: After being kicked out of the outlet mall, why would this Barry Rhodes have outbid Winston Blakely on the clock the old man was so desperate to get his hands on, and how would he have been able to afford it?

But the biggest question of all was whether or not would Barry Rhodes would have been willing to kill for it.

Chapter Twenty-two

As AMBER AND I drove back toward Honeysuckle Grove, we discussed the two men from the funeral. Percy Mahoney had been the clean-cut man in a suit, and Barry Rhodes had been the more disheveled bearded man, the one who had questioned me about the auction clock during the reception.

Now, it seemed a little clearer why since he had been the winning bidder of the grandfather clock. Although, why ask questions about it if he stole it himself? Was he there to see if one of the other bidders could have stolen it? Or was he making sure there wasn't any suspicion surrounding him?

"There is no Rhodes listed in the Juniper Mills directory," Amber said, scrolling through her phone.

I shook my head. "Alex doesn't want us to go questioning people at their houses on our own." In truth, I was the one who didn't think this was safe, but I was fairly sure Alex would back me up on it.

"Yeah, but do you think Alex has time to do it? He needs our help, but he doesn't want to ask for it. We know how to be careful." It was a decent argument, except for that last part. Only half of our investigative duo seemed to know how to be careful.

I continued to drive and not say very much to Amber's arguments. "We could just stop in and peek through some windows to see if the clock is there. Then Alex would have something to go on."

I let out a loud sigh and decided not to expend my energy on arguing. We were outside of the city limits of Juniper Mills now, and at least Amber didn't have her own car and driver's license.

Then again, that sort of thing hadn't stopped her in the past.

"Wait!" she said suddenly and so loudly I hit the brakes on instinct. Thankfully, the road was fairly empty of cars at the moment.

"Don't do that!" I told her. "You could have gotten us into an accident."

She ignored my admonishment. "There aren't any Rhodes listed in Juniper Mills, but look what else I found in the online directory?" She flashed me her phone, but I couldn't read while I was driving, so finally, she went on. "Leather Bound Shoe Shoppe. Juniper Mills, West Virginia."

I squinted at the road. "So what do you think? Did he open up a new independent shop quickly after getting kicked out of the mall? Or maybe it's a chain and there are other locations of Leather Bound stores. Maybe that's why Barry Rhodes couldn't keep up on his lease payments?"

Amber tilted her head. "Maybe. But while we're in Juniper Mills, couldn't we at least stop at this store?"

We weren't in Juniper Mills anymore, but I supposed we were a lot closer than we'd be in another hour. As I glanced at the clock on my dashboard, which now read ten to six, I suspected a free-standing store would be long closed before we got there anyway.

Better to make Amber feel like she was doing something useful so she wouldn't take off on a bus or something to break into all the suspicious stores and houses she could find on her own.

I took the next exit and turned around.

It turned out Leather Bound Shoe Shoppe was on our side of Juniper Mills and a little on the outskirts of town anyway. It didn't take us long to backtrack there, and as expected, there were no cars in the parking lot.

The shoe shop was in a free-standing round building with at least two dozen parking spots surrounding it in an arc. It was bigger than I expected, with large windows displaying boots and shoes. It gave an easy vantage point to see everything within the store, so I hoped the lack of a grandfather clock would put Amber's mind at rest.

Now that I'd seen the large building, I felt as though my suspicions that it was owned by a competitor of Barry Rhodes, and not Barry Rhodes himself, had been confirmed. But I got out of the car to follow Amber, anyway, as though we were onto a serious lead.

When we got close enough to see inside, the shoe displays in the windows were sparser than I expected. There were only three boot or shoe varieties per window, where the store owner could easily have fit twenty or more. It gave the essence of a high-end shop.

"If only we'd brought Hunch. He could probably sniff out some clues we're missing." Amber had argued all morning about bringing Hunch along, but I really didn't like leaving my cat alone in the car in the middle of winter, and we wouldn't have been able to traipse through the mall with an animal. Amber shielded her eyes with a hand and peered through each window for longer than I would have thought necessary.

Something about the displays, though, surprised me, and I pulled out my phone to find out a little more about the shoe store. I was scrolling through Yelp reviews when Amber finally finished surveying the windows and joined me, peeking over my shoulder. "What did you find?"

I shook my head. "Nothing, really. It's just surprising that this store has over five hundred reviews, and an average of 4.9 stars. I mean, what kind of business has a rating that high?"

Amber nodded. "It seems understandable if this store was at fault for putting Barry Rhodes out of business." I was glad she'd come to that conclusion on her own. "No grandfather clock inside, by the way."

I nodded and led the way back to my car. "You'd think Barry Rhodes would be angrier at the owner of this place than with Winston Blakely, right?"

Amber tilted her head back and forth. "Maybe. I think he's still worth looking into. Especially if he visited Winston's funeral. Plus, we need to find out how he planned to pay for his bid if the clock hadn't gone missing."

She was right about that. While Sheila might have thought his presence at the funeral had proven his innocence, Amber and I thought quite the opposite. The idea that the possible thief of the clock also hated Winston Blakely seemed much too coincidental for my liking. What were the chances that the clock thief and the murderer were one and the same?

I needed to talk this over with Alex, though, and not feed Amber's need to keep investigating. "For now, let's get back home and cook something up for Alex for dinner. Maybe he'll have more information about the case for us, and maybe he still wants to look into Barry Rhodes himself."

Amber didn't look completely satisfied with this plan, but at least stopping at the shoe store had garnered the desired effect and made her feel as though she'd done something useful today.

Chapter Twenty-three

ALEX WAS TOO BUSY to come for dinner, but he did call so we could give him an update. After we told him all we had learned from Sheila and about the Leather Bound store we'd stopped at on our way home, he sighed and said, "Okay, I'll get Mickey to look in on Barry Rhodes tomorrow."

I tried to quell my sigh, but Amber made a loud exclamation of hers. Alex's official partner, Mickey Bradley, was the most incompetent detective on the force, often overlooking details of cases or making quick arrests without proof.

I continued kneading dough for biscuits—a little rougher than I'd been kneading it a minute ago—but Amber stopped chopping vegetables to turn to where I had Alex on speakerphone on the counter between us. "If you're too busy to investigate Barry Rhodes, we can do it. No need to get Mickey Mouse on the job."

Hunch had been winding around Amber's legs ever since we got home, but he stopped and let out a loud *mreaow*, as if agreeing with Amber on this.

Alex was silent for a few seconds. "I don't like the idea of you two looking in on this guy without backup. If everything's leading his way, he could be dangerous."

"Dangerous, smangerous," Amber mumbled under her breath.

I hoped Alex would put it in no uncertain terms that Amber was to steer clear of Barry Rhodes, as she always seemed to take his authority as law. But instead, he changed the subject.

"In other news, I heard back from Bob, and he pegged Winston Blakely's death at 8:20 p.m."

"So during the auction?" Amber confirmed. I was glad this distracted her for the moment at least. Hunch left her side to hop onto a kitchen chair and placed a paw on my notebook of investigative details. If only he could hold a pen, he truly would be a more competent detective than all of us.

"That's right," Alex said.

"How long would it have taken to get carbon monoxide poisoning?" I snapped my mouth shut when I remembered that Winston hadn't actually died from his generator. He'd been suffocated.

But Alex's answer still helped. "In such a small room, it would have only taken minutes, definitely less than half an hour. So we can safely assume that he was asphyxiated after eight and then the generator placed inside his office. The person responsible could have easily been gone from his property by eight thirty."

"Is there a way to check what time Jackie Reed was actually on a plane?" Amber asked. "She said eight, which would put her in the clear, especially with having to drive to an airport from here, but if her flight wasn't actually until nine or ten, she could still be a suspect."

"Good idea." Alex's positivity was almost completely masked by his exhaustion. "I'll put that on my list to check into tomorrow."

I felt the need to jump on this and show Amber how helpful she was being from right here in my kitchen. No need to go physically chasing after murder suspects. "In the meantime, we could call the Mardi Gras Hotel in Las Vegas and see what time anyone can place Jackie Reed there on the night Winston was killed, if they can place her at all."

I still didn't think Jackie Reed was guilty of killing her late boyfriend, but this would at least keep Amber and me busy this evening. If Jackie indeed had the job she claimed with her parents' hotel, it would be unlikely she'd been after Winston's money.

After hanging up, Amber returned to chopping vegetables and quickly returned to the topic of Barry Rhodes. "Chad from the antique store was supposed to have delivered the grandfather clock, right? He must have an address for Barry Rhodes."

Amber had searched the Internet three times for an address for a Barry Rhodes in or around Juniper Mills, West Virginia, but hadn't come up with any matches. My dad always used to say that only a person with something to hide kept themselves as unlisted in the local phone book. Of course, a lot of people didn't have landlines anymore, and I didn't listen to much of what my dad told me, but this was one tidbit that stuck with me.

I sighed. "We're not going to go confront a murder suspect at his house," I told Amber, trying to sound resolute, even though I wanted to help solve this case as much as she did. "Especially when Alex expressly told us not to."

Amber had moved on to cubing some chicken breasts to make one of her delicious stir-frys, but she stopped what she was doing and held out her hands, as though showing me the chicken slime covering them. "I'm not saying we need to confront the guy. But while he's at work or whatever, we could sneak in and look around for that grandfather clock. If he has it, that would be enough evidence to at least bring him in for questioning."

She had a point, but it still sounded too dangerous. I had another idea. "How about instead we start with visiting that Leather Bound store while it's open tomorrow?" I liked the idea of being in a public store during business hours. What could happen to us, especially if there were other customers? "We'll ask the owner what he or she knows about Barry Rhodes, and that might inform us better about how to move forward with investigating him." She still looked downtrodden about it, so I hit her with my last selling point. "We'll even bring Hunch."

I expected the owner to at least know Barry by name. Perhaps there would have been some animosity between them. Amber seemed satisfied that I was willing to take her back to Juniper Mills tomorrow. I figured she'd prod me in the morning to stop by Chad's Antique Village to try and get an address for Barry Rhodes. I wasn't great at fighting off Amber's agenda when she seemed to have a one-track mind, but I hoped I'd be able to put up a good argument with twelve hours to prepare myself.

But then something else occurred to me. "Wait, tomorrow's Monday! You have school." This argument was such a common one, it should've been on the tip of my tongue.

Amber only waved a casual hand with her spatula. "I'll do it tonight. Mom's letting me do all my courses online now, remember? It's more work, but at least I can do it when I want."

I squinted at her. Too often she bent the truth to get away with things. "I'll need you to show me that every bit of your schoolwork is done or you're not going anywhere."

She shrugged and turned back to her cooking. "Sure. No prob."

The no-prob answer had been more casual and laid-back than the truth of the matter. After dinner, I cleaned up the dishes while Amber worked on her laptop at my kitchen table, not even looking away from the screen to methodically pet Hunch.

She stayed there while I tidied the living room and cleaned both bathrooms. Finally, I was too antsy to stay away from working on the case any longer, even if I had to do it on my own. I'd always thought Amber was the eager one when it came to investigating, so it surprised me that when she was forced to back off and I didn't feel the need to corral her, my own eagerness reared its head.

I took my laptop and cell phone up to my bedroom. Amber didn't seem to even notice me leaving the room, so wrapped up in a complicated biology video that streamed through her headphones.

After setting up my laptop and cell phone on my nightstand, I layered three pillows against my headboard to settle in. Hunch nudged my bedroom door open, apparently having kitty intuition that I was about to work on the case. This would be much more exciting to him than biology or even Amber's affection.

Before getting comfortable, I shut my bedroom door behind him. No need for my voice to stream downstairs and interrupt Amber's concentration.

The Mardi Gras Hotel and Casino in Las Vegas was not difficult to find. With a little research, I quickly discovered that the structure had been a landmark in Las Vegas for almost fifty years, although it had worn several different names over that time. A little further research revealed that the hotel was just off the main strip in Las Vegas, a favorite of locals, and had been owned by Owen and Tabitha Reed for the last decade.

The fact that the owners shared a last name with Jackie certainly felt as though it corroborated her story, but I had to make sure.

Under Contact Information, there were three main phone numbers: one for events, one for the casino, and one for the hotel. I picked up my cell phone and dialed the one for the hotel, glad that tonight's research wasn't going to be rushed by business hours.

A young-sounding man picked up after only a couple of rings. "Mardi Gras Hotel and Casino. How may I direct your call?"

"Hi there. May I speak to Owen or Tabitha Reed, please?" I said, reading their names off my laptop screen.

"I'm afraid Mr. Reed isn't in at the moment, and I think..." After a short pause, he returned to the line. "Yes, the spa is closed for the evening, so you won't be able to catch Mrs. Reed either. May I take a message?"

After I had settled into the bedroom and was ready to make some headway on this case, this young man was shutting me down far too quickly. A tenaciousness rose up within me.

"I'm a special consultant with a police department in West Virginia. I have a few questions, and they are fairly urgent. Are you sure you can't get me in touch with one of the Reeds?"

"No, ma'am. I'm afraid they can't be reached after hours." The young man was unfazed by my mention of the police, which made me wonder how often this sort of pressure was put upon him.

"Well, can I speak to your manager, then?" I was still upright on the edge of my bed, unable to settle in when it seemed no answers would be forthcoming. Hunch sat beside me on his haunches, staring at my open laptop, as if reading all about the Mardi Gras Hotel and Casino.

"I'm the night desk manager, ma'am." I didn't like the way he said ma'am, as though I was more of an annoyance than a valued customer. Then again, I'd made clear I was not a customer. "If there's anything I can help you with, I'd be more than happy to." His offer sounded less than genuine.

"And your name is?" I asked, trying to find the upper hand in the conversation.

"Jeremy Estevez." He gave the name easily, without pause. He didn't seem bothered that I might report him to his boss, which somehow bothered me even more.

"Well, Mr. Estevez, the Honeysuckle Police Department is investigating the whereabouts of a Miss Jackie Reed on the evening of December thirty-first. Can you help me with that?"

My tone was snotty and a little condescending, so it surprised me when he said, "Jackie? Well, sure. Of course."

"You can?"

I could hear him typing on a computer in the background. "We weren't expecting Jackie that night. It was a little crazy in the casino, as you can imagine on New Year's Eve in a casino in Vegas." I couldn't really imagine, but he went on casually, not needing any prodding. "I hear that poor girl had to drop everything and fly across the country because Cathy had overbooked the hotel with a convention she thought was only using our theater. It was some mess by the time I came on shift that evening."

"And what time did you come on shift?" I asked.

"Nine p.m. Same as always."

"And did you see Jackie when you came on shift at nine?" I asked.

I could practically see him shaking his head on the other end of the line. "My first job of the night was arranging a car to pick her up at the airport at midnight."

This certainly seemed to corroborate that Jackie was a woman of means, if nothing else. "And exactly what time was her flight arriving?" As I asked the question, I looked up the travel time between Charleston and Las Vegas. Just under four hours.

"I believe it would have been eleven forty-five," he told me.

With the drive to Charleston, it seemed unlikely that Jackie could have smothered Winston, set up the generator, got to the airport and then to Las Vegas to fix the hotel's mix-ups.

Unlikely. But not impossible. Especially if this guy was fudging the truth for his boss.

"And can you tell me what time you saw Miss Reed that night, and how she seemed?"

"Oh, she was frazzled and annoyed, and who would blame her? It was probably three a.m. before she actually came out of the offices and took a breath. She'd been spending a boatload of hotel money and rebooking disgruntled guests wherever she could find places around town. She had to comp them rooms, meals, even limos to try and appease them, and all because of an oversight of Cathy's. Believe me, we all miss having Jackie around here and will be glad to have her back."

I wondered if they missed having her around enough to lie for her.

But that wasn't really the point, I decided as I thanked Jeremy Estevez for his help and hung up. The point was that I hadn't been able to take anything off Alex's very full plate, after all. Even as a special consultant, I wouldn't be able to find out exactly which flight Jackie Reed had been on, but Alex would.

Chapter Twenty-four

THE NEXT MORNING, AMBER must have been up with the birds because there were fresh blueberry scones and a sizzling cheesy bacon scramble ready to eat by the time I arrived in my kitchen.

"Mmm, smells delicious."

She looked up from where she was nibbling on a scone behind her laptop at the table.

"Did you get your schoolwork done?" I should have probably asked her if she even went to bed.

She nodded. "Almost. Just one more lab report to submit." She took a bite of her scone, which caused my stomach to rumble.

I helped myself to a large enough plate for a healthy serving of scramble and a scone. Amber had started drinking coffee since her sixteenth birthday. So far I hadn't commented on it. With the amount of milk and sugar she added, I wasn't sure the caffeine would be a problem. But I suspected she didn't know how to use my coffee maker, as she never made any before I was up.

I hesitated, thinking maybe we should both try and kick the caffeine habit, but then decided today was not the day. She clearly didn't have a problem getting her brain into gear first thing in the morning. I needed a little help in that department.

By the time I had my full coffee cup and plate of food ready to eat for breakfast, Amber slapped the lid of her laptop shut, leaving me with no question about where I should sit to eat.

"Done?" I asked.

"Done." She offered me a tired smile. But only a second later, the tiredness evaporated when she asked, "So what's our plan for today? Going to Chad's to get an address for Barry Rhodes, then the Leather Bound store, and then what?"

At the mention of the investigation, Hunch made his way from his food dish and wound around Amber's legs until she picked him up.

I nodded. "Chad's doesn't open until nine, so we'd have to wait until then to ask him where he planned to deliver the grandfather clock."

Her eyes widened with excitement. "So you do want to search his place?"

I put my plate and coffee cup across from her and pressed both hands toward the floor. "Calm down. I just think it's good to have some information before we drive all the way to Juniper Mills." I hadn't come up with a way to divert Amber from this and had planned to mention stopping at Chad's before we left town more discreetly, but of course, I hadn't had my first sip of coffee yet. "Maybe Chad has a phone number for Mr. Rhodes," I said, trying to backtrack.

Amber rolled her eyes at my mention of using the phone to track down our suspect. But she didn't argue. She must have appreciated that my willingness to look into the guy had improved since last night. The only thing I could account for this was the fact that I'd wanted so badly to clear Jackie Reed from suspicion the night before, just to be of some help.

I told Amber about my conversation with Jeremy Estevez. Her attention was rapt on my every word.

"So Jackie was on a plane while Winston was being murdered?" she asked as soon as I finished recounting the conversation.

"Maybe. Probably. But I still have to get Alex to look into the flight manifests to make sure. I'm not convinced that the staff at her parents' hotel wouldn't stretch the truth for her."

Amber pulled the lid up on her computer again. "Or we can just check the flight times."

"Already did," I told her. "It's just under four hours between Charleston and Las Vegas, so that's why the time is iffy."

Her hands flew over her keyboard as if I hadn't spoken. "No, I mean what time the flights left from Charleston. If she was getting picked up anytime even close to midnight, she would have had to leave out of Charleston by eight."

I stopped eating and went to watch over Amber's shoulder. Hunch put a paw on the edge of her laptop as though he was going to help with the search. Soon, Amber had the flight times on New Year's Eve listed.

"There were flights at four fifteen and seven fifty-eight. Nothing else until the next day." Amber looked up at me, confirming that she'd just cleared Jackie Reed, but I thought of something else.

"What about other airports? Or what about connecting flights?"

She raised her eyebrows as if I was reaching. And I was. But after only a few seconds of Amber's furious typing, we had our answer. Pittsburgh would be her next closest choice to get to Las Vegas, and with the driving distance, that would definitely put her outside of the killing time zone. Any connecting flights left far too much of a time gap.

"So that's it," I said. "Jackie Reed is off our list."

I still planned on calling the business school in Detroit to confirm that she had been in touch about donating Winston's money, but at this point, that could wait until later.

I sat across from Amber again and pulled my notepad closer, crossing Jackie off my list of suspects.

She packed up her laptop. "Well, for now, I think Barry Rhodes is our best bet. Let's get to Juniper Mills and see what we can find out about the guy."

Chapter Twenty-five

CHAD'S ANTIQUE VILLAGE WAS much slower on a Monday morning than it had been on a Sunday. Amber and I strode straight for his counter and surprised Chad, as we usually did. I wondered if he was starting to lose his hearing.

"Morning, Chad," I called from a distance, hoping he wouldn't drop anything at our voices.

He didn't. As soon as he looked up and recognized us, a smile spread across his face. Amber had packed up a few raspberry scones for him and passed them across the counter. "We brought these in case you hadn't had breakfast."

"Well, I've had breakfast, but that would never stop me from eating something you baked up for me."

Amber beamed at the compliment and then got straight to the point. "We're following up on some details of the missing grandfather clock for Detective Martinez." Amber was always much bolder in grouping us with official police proceedings than I was. "We need an address for Barry Rhodes. We want to pay him a surprise visit to ask a few questions."

Chad's forehead creased, and despite the scone in his hand that he had almost at his mouth, he became instantly serious. "I already told Mallory that I'm afraid he's not in my system. He hasn't been a regular client."

"But don't you have a delivery address for the grandfather clock?" Amber pushed.

He nibbled his lip, and a second later, he snapped his fingers. "The van's manifest! I hadn't even thought of that."

He opened his laptop on the counter and explained as he started scrolling. "I have a list of everything that was in the van, grouped into sections of where it was to be delivered. All the items that didn't sell came back here, but you're right. There must have been an address for Barry Rhodes's delivery on there."

We waited him out while he pulled his glasses down on his nose and looked closer at his screen. "It looks like I have two addresses for him. His home address to bill his credit card, but the clock was supposed to be delivered to his shop. Which address would you like?"

"His shop?" So Barry Rhodes had already opened another shop since getting evicted from Juniper Mills outlet mall?

Chad nodded as Amber said, "Why don't you give us both."

Amber and I took note as he rattled off an unfamiliar house address in Juniper Mills. Then he said, "And his shop where we were supposed to deliver the clock is called Leather Bound. It's right off the highway near Juniper Mills." He gave us the exact address, not noticing that both Amber and I had stopped writing to stare at each other.

"*That* shop belongs to Barry Rhodes?" I confirmed. "We stopped there yesterday, and it was already closed, but it looked like a really successful business."

Chad tilted his head. "I suppose it would have to be for him to be able to afford the grandfather clock."

True. So much for my theory that he'd stolen the clock because he didn't have the money to cover his bid. "And you were supposed to deliver it to his store that night?" I asked.

Chad shook his head. "I'd arranged a parking spot at Pelton Storage overnight. They have a security guard, so because of the late hour, I planned to keep the items for delivery and those that didn't sell, and then deliver them the next day."

Something wasn't adding up. But I supposed we were more likely to find the inconsistency in Juniper Mills than here in

Chad's Antique Village. We thanked Chad and headed for my car.

Thankfully, there wasn't much snow left on the highway on the drive out of town. Amber and I discussed the suspects of the case, with Hunch at attention on her lap.

"So Jackie Reed had an alibi," Amber said, reading from my notepad. "And so did Roland Conway, at least for the most part. What about Sheila Blakely? She was at the auction, but she also seems to lie a lot or, at the very least, tell us half-truths."

"But could she have killed her own father?" Before Amber could answer and remind me that often murderers did not seem like murderers, and sometimes close relationships brought out the most passionate of reactions, I added, "And you're right, she was in our view at the auction the whole evening."

"What time did she arrive?" Amber asked, flipping through my notepad to see if I'd written anything down in that regard.

I hadn't. But after repeatedly going over the details of that night in my mind, I had a pretty good memory. "She came in while we were still setting up, so before seven thirty. At first, the only thing I noticed about her was her belly, but as time went on and the community center filled, her stress level over her father's absence became the most noticeable thing about her. She would not have had time to smother her father, and even if she had the strength to move the generator, I don't think she'd have been able to handle maneuvering it in her state. What bothers me is why Sheila didn't immediately tell me she blamed Jackie. Why was she so sneaky about that?"

Amber shrugged. "Maybe she didn't really suspect Jackie, but it seemed like an opportunity to yell at the woman who had monopolized all her dad's time?" she guessed. "Or maybe she thought she'd have a better chance of contesting her dad's will if there was some guilt shed toward the main beneficiary."

"Or maybe..." I spoke the thought as it occurred to me. "What if Sheila was covering for her boyfriend? What if she was redirecting suspicion, and that's why she kept it so quiet initially?"

Amber nibbled her lip. "I dunno. I don't get the feeling Dylan could kill anybody."

I looked away from the road for a second to raise my eyebrows. My retort didn't need to be voiced because with every murder investigation we'd helped solve up until that point, we hadn't been able to see the murderer as being capable of killing anybody.

Amber didn't like my eyebrow rebuttal, and the truth was, the more I'd spoken to the guy, the more I'd started to like him, too. But I had to put my feelings aside and look only at the evidence.

"We didn't see him until just before the auction started, and he didn't stick around long. He didn't have much love for his soon-to-be father-in-law, so he had motive. Plus, he would've had the strength to move the generator, so means, and his only alibi for the time during the auction is his work at the alpaca farm and then his neighbors who could only account for his presence around midnight. What was the name of his employer at the alpaca farm?"

Amber flipped pages until she found it in my notes. "Mr. Hakim."

I nodded. "It might be worth making a phone call to Mr. Hakim once we've visited the Leather Bound shop."

"What do you think about their shotgun wedding?" Amber asked. "I mean, they weren't planning to get married until just after the funeral. Isn't that weird?"

I nodded. "I wonder if we should talk to Jackie before she leaves town and ask her if she has any intel on what Winston had thought about his daughter marrying Dylan. She did say there were specific notes in his will about the raising of his grandchild." I had a feeling the cutthroat businessman didn't have a lot of love for his daughter's boyfriend, the alpaca farmer.

"Hmm." Amber looked through my notes and moved along to the next suspect. "Or there's Barry Rhodes, who bid on and won the clock that Winston had been going on about nonstop for months. Barry was angry at Winston for kicking him out of the outlet mall, so he had motive. The generator was on wheels, so he would have been able to move it. That gives him the means."

I wanted to temper her enthusiasm on this one for fear she might barrel into the Leather Bound store with slanderous words launching out of her mouth before we were even through the door. "Yes, but that could probably be said for a handful of business owners from Juniper Mills."

Amber went on as if I hadn't spoken. "He phoned in his bid, so as far as we know, he has no alibi."

"We haven't even asked him that yet, so let's not jump to conclusions."

Amber rolled her eyes, but at least she didn't argue. We went through all of the suspects once again, Amber reading off the pertinent information from my notebook.

If I didn't feel as though Dylan was the person responsible in my gut, I supposed I should probably also focus on trying to pin this on Barry Rhodes.

I just wasn't sure I believed that either.

Chapter Twenty-six

WE PULLED INTO THE Leather Bound parking lot just after eleven. It had been hard to get a definite reading on the store's success yesterday, but not today. The parking lot was so crowded, we ended up grabbing the last available parking spot.

Their inventory had to be low because they were selling so much so quickly. Either that or they were the type of high-end establishment that prided themselves on spacing out their items more than necessary.

Both Amber and I furrowed our brows as we walked toward the front door. Once inside, I looked from the lineup of a dozen people at the till to several more customers scattered around the showroom perusing the footwear. An iPad was set up right near the door with a sign that read: "Our valued customers – please sign up for our email list so we can stay in touch about new arrivals. Every email address will be entered into a monthly draw to win a free pair of Leather Bound shoes!"

One salesman busily rang up orders while the other helped a couple near a front window, but even while the place seemed understaffed, there was a feeling of leisure throughout the shop. No customer seemed in a hurry. It felt as though everyone here knew it could be an all-day event to purchase a pair of Leather Bound shoes.

Amber, however, did not feel as though she had all day. She marched toward the salesman on the floor, crossed her arms, and tapped her foot impatiently.

The salesman couldn't have been more than five-six in weathered jeans and a dress shirt. He must have felt Amber's eager energy because he kept glancing away from the couple he was helping to offer her reassuring smiles that he knew she was there and he would be with her shortly.

It only took me a few seconds and one or two calming breaths to remember that Amber was the one with her priorities straight. I was often too afraid of embarrassing myself and tended to forget that our objective was investigating a murder. Certainly, we should be able to call a salesman away from his current business for that.

I crossed the store and stood beside Amber, now resolute. With two of us radiating agitated energy, the salesman quickly left the couple with two pairs of shoes to try on their own and then moved a few feet away from them, likely trying to pull our anxious energy away so they could relax and shop.

"What can I help you with?" The salesman's name tag read: MARTIN. While Martin's voice had been soothing with the couple he'd been helping, it quickly adopted an all-business tone for us, as though he knew this was serious.

"We're looking for Barry Rhodes." Amber dug her fists into her waist. "Is he in?"

I glanced around the store for the bearded man I'd spoken to at the funeral. He didn't appear to be here.

When I looked back, the salesman shook his head. "He's off on Mondays."

"But he does own this store?" I asked.

Martin nodded, but his jaw seemed to hold more tension by the second. I suddenly wondered if his tone hadn't only become more serious. It had become more defensive.

"How long has this location been open?" Amber asked, not giving him a chance to elaborate if he wanted to.

Martin looked up, thinking. "Six months. Now, I'm sure you've noticed we're very busy. If you're not here to purchase footwear, I'll have to ask you to leave."

Definitely defensive. It was time to pull out the big guns. "My name is Mallory Beck, and I'm a special consultant with the Honeysuckle Grove Police Department. We're currently investigating some information on a recent case. Believe me when I tell you it would be in your best interest to answer my questions now, rather than having to be dragged into another town's police station." I'd heard Alex use this kind of threat before. It definitely didn't sound as natural coming out of my mouth, but at least it had the desired effect.

His eyebrows furrowed. "What kind of case?"

Before Amber could insert the word "murder" full of her usual drama, I nipped this one in the bud. "That's none of your concern right now. What is your concern is telling us everything you know about your boss's dealings with a Mr. Winston Blakely."

His forehead buckled even more. "Blakely? Well, he kicked Barry out of the mall, but that was months ago. As far as I know, they haven't seen each other since."

"Winston Blakely has never been into this store location, to your knowledge?" Amber asked.

Martin shook his head.

"How did your boss feel toward Mr. Blakely?" I asked.

"How would you feel if your thriving business got kicked out of its location for no good reason? Barry used to use his name as a slight whenever one of us did something stupid. He'd say, 'Don't be a Winston.'"

I tilted my head. "For no good reason? And you said the business was thriving? I was under the impression he was kicked out of the mall for not keeping up with his lease payments?"

Martin's eyebrows shot up high on his forehead. He motioned to the busy store around us. "Do you really think that was the case?"

"If not for money, why would Winston Blakely have kicked him out?" Amber asked the question I was thinking.

Martin shook his head. "I couldn't tell you for sure, but we all think," he motioned toward the salesman at the till, "that it was after that showgirl of Blakely's started hanging around. She was way too young for Blakely. Definitely more Barry's age, and she came into the store to talk to Barry regularly. Next thing I knew, there was a big yelling match between Barry and Blakely. We kept to our business and couldn't hear much of what was said, except Barry said something about showing Blakely what's what. Barry came back into the store all beet-red and said he needed us all in to work that Sunday to move all of his stock to a new, better location." He looked around the store. "I have to admit, this place really does suit our clientele better."

"How so?" I asked.

"There's so much more room here. People have the time and space to spend an afternoon deciding on their new footwear. It never felt quite right in a hurried outlet mall."

"How long have you been with the company?" I asked.

"Since Barry started it two years ago," he told me. "Barry's very loyal to his employees. Gives us regular raises, treats us well."

Through Martin's eyes, Barry Rhodes certainly didn't sound like a murderer or someone who needed to steal anything. But I reminded myself that didn't necessarily mean anything.

"Were you aware of Mr. Rhodes bidding on an antique grandfather clock recently?" I asked.

Martin shook his head. "I don't think so. Why?"

I decided we may as well show our cards on this one. Perhaps it would stir up some sort of truth we were missing. "On New Year's Eve, Barry Rhodes bid on and won an antique clock that apparently Winston Blakely had been eager to purchase."

A smile edged onto Martin's face. It wasn't until he spoke when I remembered Martin didn't know the seriousness of the situation. He probably didn't even know Winston had died. "Barry outbid Blakely?" He whistled. "That must have killed the old man."

For a second, I was stunned into silence by his turn of phrase. Amber, however, was not. "You could say that. Does it surprise you that they were competitive over an antique clock?"

"Heh. It doesn't surprise me that Barry would have challenged Blakely on anything. When he first kicked him out of the mall, Barry went on for weeks about how he planned to get back at Winston Blakely."

"Did he give any specifics on what he planned to do?" I asked, trying not to show my shock.

Martin shook his head. "Just that he planned to put his whole mall out of business. For a couple of weeks, he tried to get in touch with others who'd had their businesses kicked out of the mall, but then he came back into the store in a huff one day, telling us that Winston Blakely had moved away to some little town to hide away from all the people who hated him most. We never heard much more about Blakely after that. Except when any of us called each other a Winston." Martin let out a low chuckle.

"You don't happen to know Mr. Rhodes' whereabouts on New Year's Eve?"

Martin shrugged. "I invited him to a friend's get-together, but he said he'd be busy at home, buying himself a special gift." Martin raised an eyebrow. "Was that the clock?" Before I could answer, Martin tilted his head in thought. "Surprising he wouldn't bring it into the store and flaunt it."

Not surprising to us, of course, but I didn't need to get into all of that. As Amber spoke, I could feel her agitated energy again. She was clearly done here. "Do you know where Mr. Rhodes is today? Is he at his house in Juniper Mills?"

But as Martin nodded and said, "Probably," I didn't feel any closer to knowing whether or not Barry Rhodes had killed Winston Blakely, and I most certainly did not want to track him down on his own isolated turf.

Chapter Twenty-seven

AMBER SEEMED TO KNOW how dead set I would be against bombarding Barry Rhodes at his house. The second we were out of the shoe shop, she argued with me about it as though I'd already told her we couldn't go there.

"He's obviously guilty. He was home alone the night Winston Blakely was killed." She ticked items off on her fingers. "He hated the guy. He had the ability to move a generator. What if that Martin guy tips him off before the police can get to him?"

She had a point there.

I was about to get into my car when my phone buzzed from my purse. I pulled it out and quickly answered when I saw it was Alex. "What's up?"

"I was just calling to see how everything was going on your end. I'm just about to head out to get an update from the medical examiner. Did you drive into Juniper Mills?" As usual, he sounded tired.

I nodded, even though he wouldn't be able to see it, and recounted all we'd discovered from Martin the Salesman. "Amber wants to go to Barry Rhodes's house next to confront him, but I told her it's too dangerous."

Amber had moved beside me, outside my car, the second she realized it was Alex on the phone. Poor Hunch was trapped inside, pawing at the window, wanting to hear, but I stood stock still, holding my breath and hoping Alex wasn't too tired to realize I needed him to back me up on this.

I heard him typing in the background, which meant he was likely at the police station. Finally, he said, "Let me get a hold of Juniper Mills P.D. and see if they can send someone over there. I'd still like you two to go, as you know a lot better than them what questions to ask, but I don't want you doing it without backup."

I shouldn't have doubted Alex. Even at his most exhausted, he never seemed to lack investigative smarts. "Okay, great. So you'll get back to us and let us know?"

Amber ducked her face closer to my phone. "We'll head over there and stake out the place to make sure he doesn't leave."

Clearly distracted, Alex said, "Sounds good," and then promised he'd call us with an update soon before hanging up.

Me? I was nervous about taking Amber any closer to this Rhodes suspect. She tended to barrel through life without considering the consequences. More than once in prior investigations, her impulsive actions had put her life in danger, and even Alex got injured in our last one. What if she jumped out of my car and headed for his house before I had word that the police were on their way?

I insisted on stopping for coffee and drove slowly toward Barry Rhodes' house. I looped around the block, claiming to want to get the lay of the land before the police arrived. I could rely on these sorts of excuses when I was behind the wheel. Now that Amber was sixteen, I dreaded the day when she'd have her license and the ability to make her own investigative decisions without any safety precautions or backup. I hoped I could talk some sense into her or at the very least demonstrate balanced investigative behavior before that happened.

By the time I'd looped around the suburban neighborhood where Barry Rhodes lived, my phone pinged with a text from Alex.

~Police are on their way.~

Short and sweet, which likely meant he was too busy to talk. I wondered if he was at the medical examiner's office already. I wondered if Bob Shone had new information that could help us prove Barry Rhodes' guilt. Another text popped up on my screen.

~They'll stay on the street unless you need help.~

I pulled up against the curb, just down from Barry's one-story ranch-style house, and wondered if that meant Alex thought we weren't in any real danger. Or maybe the Juniper Mills Police Department just wasn't the type to go out of their way to help.

"You're not really going to wait in the car, right?" Amber asked, her eyebrows raised. "Now that we know they're coming."

I looked around. In truth, the neighborhood seemed safe enough, with houses surrounding us on every side. If we remained outside to question him, we'd be in view of a dozen houses, many of which had cars in their driveways. A yell for help wouldn't be missed around here. I was pretty sure of it.

But I still stalled, taking a sip of my coffee, double-checking my phone, and making sure my notepad page was flipped and ready for more notes.

Amber already stood outside my car, tapping her foot impatiently. She had Hunch in her arms, and while it wouldn't look as professional to the Juniper Mills P.D. to have a cat on the job, I wasn't opposed to her bringing him along for this particular interview.

We walked up the front walk toward Barry's house, and my anxiety was further calmed when a Volkswagen pulled up behind us and into the neighboring driveway. A clean-cut man in a suit got out, smiled, nodded in our direction, and then headed to his own front door. The area wasn't deserted. How dangerous could this be?

As if Amber could read my mind, she strode straight for Barry's door and rang the bell without waiting to see if I was ready. We'd come up with a few questions to ask while looping around the block, but I hoped Amber would wait with the hard-hitting ones until the police arrived.

We heard footsteps, and a few seconds later, the door swung open to a man I immediately recognized. Barry Rhodes was definitely the man with the unkempt beard from Winston's funeral. That seemed as good a place as any to start, and because I didn't want Amber jumping in and accusing him of murder right off the bat, I quickly held out a hand and said, "Barry Rhodes? I recognize you from Winston Blakely's funeral service."

Barry visibly winced at Winston's name, but recovered quickly and shook my hand. "You were friends with Blakely?"

I shook my head. "We actually catered the event, remember? We'd never met the man."

This statement seemed to relax Barry, but no sooner had that happened than Amber said, "But today we're here as special consultants with the Honeysuckle Grove Police Department." She left what was probably supposed to be a dramatic pause, but Barry only looked from Amber to the cat in her arms, confused.

"We're filling in some details of an investigation," I explained.

"What? They have a lead on my clock?" I didn't think he was faking the eagerness in his voice, but I couldn't be sure.

"No, the investigation surrounding Mr. Blakely's death," Amber said, deadpan.

Now he looked between us, his forehead buckled. "Investigation?"

His reaction seemed genuine, but I only answered his question with one of my own. "Can you tell us where you were on the evening of December thirty-first?"

"New Year's Eve? Sure, right here at home." He looked between the two of us. "Why?"

Before I could open my mouth, Amber said, "They've upgraded the case of Winston Blakely's death to murder. Do you have anyone who can account for your presence that night?"

Barry pulled back, realization shrouding his face. "Wait, you don't think..." He looked in both directions. "I was here all night! Just ask Brad and Susan." He motioned to the neighbor's house where we'd just seen a man go inside. "Or Harry." He motioned across the street.

"They would have actually seen you and been able to account for your presence that entire evening?"

He nodded, and his face appeared open. "I was helping Brad with the tri-tips on the barbecue all night. He's got a covered deck with propane heaters," he explained and then added before I could even question him on the time, "Got over there by six o'clock."

But Amber, as always, was on top of the inconsistencies. "So you didn't bid on an antique clock that night?"

His gaze darted to Amber, but he looked back at me before he answered. "I did..." He drew out the word, and I held my breath, waiting for more. "I called in a bid from out on Brad's back patio. He was there with me," Barry added when we didn't immediately respond.

"Why phone in a bid if you wanted the clock so bad?" Amber asked. Thankfully, she was on top of the smart questions.

Barry nodded and finally looked at her as he answered. "I wanted to. I had the money to outbid Blakely, I was sure of it. And I wanted to see his face when it happened. But Brad talked me down. He said it'd be even more effective if I won the bid by phone. He told me to imagine Blakely seething at the auction and not having anywhere to direct his anger and frustration. Plus, the weather was awful. At the time, of course, I'd had no idea Blakely wasn't even there. It's no wonder I got the clock so cheap."

"Did you only want the clock because Winston Blakely wanted it?" Another great question from Amber. "Or was it an antique you were actually interested in?" She let Hunch down out of her arms. He immediately sniffed the air around him and then moved closer to Barry to sniff the leg of his weathered jeans.

Barry looked down, seemingly sheepish for the first time during this conversation. "I had to do something to show the old man he hadn't bested me." Barry seemed to realize his poor phrasing and looked up quickly. "I mean, I'd never have physically hurt the old guy, but ever since he canceled my lease with no notice and kicked me out of the mall with no good reason, I just wanted to make a public show that the old man couldn't have everything just because he wanted it."

"Were you ever late on your lease payments?" I asked, still surprised at the "no good reason" explanation.

He shook his head. "Not once. I was a model tenant."

Hunch nosed past him and sniffed inside his house. I sure hoped I wasn't going to have to go in there after my cat. Even though Barry Rhodes seemed to have an alibi for New Year's Eve, I still wasn't sure I trusted him enough to go inside his house.

Amber squinted at him. "From everything I've heard, Winston Blakely was an astute businessman. Why would he have kicked out a well-paying, compliant tenant from his mall? What did you do?" Amber was great with her bold questions—sometimes too bold for my comfort, but she knew how not to let suspects out of answering.

Barry took in a deep breath and let it out in a sigh. "His woman kept coming in my store. She was really flirty, and I admit, I didn't mind the attention. I didn't even mind how angry it seemed to make that grumpy old guy. My staff all joked about it. At least until he canceled my lease."

"This was Jackie Reed?" I confirmed. When he nodded, I asked, "Did you ever actually go out with her? Did anything physical happen between the two of you?"

He let out a humorless laugh. "No. But Blakely thought something had for sure, and I guess who could blame him when his woman came back with a new pair of my shoes every day one week." He raised his eyebrows. "Leather Bound shoes are well made, for sure, but they're not cheap."

That part was true. I'd seen the price tags on some of the shoes in his store.

"Okay, so he kicked you out of his mall six months ago, and you've been holding a grudge against Mr. Blakely this whole time?" Amber asked. We would most certainly check with Brad from next door about Barry's alibi, but in the meantime, Amber was fixated on Barry's motive.

"Wouldn't you?" Barry glanced down when Hunch returned from inside his house, gave his legs one more quick sniff, and then perched on his haunches at Amber's feet, apparently done with his investigation. "The guy could have ruined my business completely if one of my salesmen didn't have a brother in real estate who had come across an empty commercial building just outside of town and if I hadn't been diligent about keeping a mailing list of all my customers." I recalled the iPad near the door of the Leather Bound shop. "We were up and running again within a week. I held a special sale, which I never usually hold sales, and it worked like a charm to keep my shoe store alive. In fact, it's thriving more now than it was in the mall."

I didn't doubt that. "You never held sales, even when you were located in an outlet mall?" Even though this was inconsequential, my mind automatically gravitated to any inconsistencies, no matter how small they might seem.

Barry tilted his head back and forth. "There were a lot of shops in there that weren't actually outlet stores. Because the mall brought in a high class of foot traffic, though, people looking for high-end brand names, lots of little independent stores make a good profit in there, too. Or they did until Blakely started kicking them out."

"He kicked them out just because they were independent?" Amber asked.

"Well, with most of them, he let their leases run out and then wouldn't renew them. He was all about getting more of the big brand names in there, ever since he bought the mall three years ago."

"So did you suspect it was only a matter of time before he kicked you out, even without the flirting of Miss Reed?" I asked.

Barry shook his head. "The shoe shop was bringing customers to his mall. We'd gained a following. I thought he'd have to be crazy to kick us out. My shoe store wasn't like that sushi place that no one went to in winter or the artisan shop with carved and woven goods that always sat empty. We had people driving from out of state to our store. Sometimes we had a lineup outside the store first thing in the mornings."

Amber went back to the subject of the clock, still poking at any inconsistencies. "We understand you've been badgering the police about the missing grandfather clock. Why do you care so much now that Mr. Blakely's not even around to see you get it?"

I hadn't thought about that. Amber's mind was often like a complicated maze of wired connections.

"I don't care about the stupid clock," Barry said, surprising us. "The guy at the antique shop already charged my credit card. He said he can't refund my money until he either gets the clock back or his insurance pays out. To be honest, I figured Blakely had sent someone out to steal it after he lost the bid, but the police said they can't find any evidence of the clock anywhere near his place. I guess I went to his funeral because part of me thought it was only a ruse, and the old man was hiding away somewhere with my expensive clock. But I saw his dead body with my very own eyes. I'm just not about to lose twenty-five grand over a clock I didn't even want."

That made sense. I glanced at Amber, but she looked back at me, as though she was out of questions. Hunch licked at one of his paws, also out of interest in this interview. That should have told me something.

But I had one final question I always asked suspects, and I wouldn't leave until I had a truthful answer to this one. "If you didn't physically harm Winston Blakely on New Year's Eve, who do you think would have done it?"

Barry shrugged. "I don't know. That woman of his, Jackie? She would have gotten his money, right?"

I shook my head. "She was out of town at the time." I didn't feel the need to fill him in on Jackie's money situation. Amber had made a call to the business school in Michigan on our drive into Juniper Mills, and her story about gifting Winston's money to the school in the form of a building fund checked out. "Who else?"

He shrugged again, but then something occurred to him, and he let out a humorless laugh. "You know that artisan shop I was telling you about? The one that got kicked out of the mall?" When we both nodded, he went on. "The owner had a yelling match with Blakely, right in the middle of the day while the mall was open. From what I hear, the guy wasn't as lucky about finding a prime piece of real estate as me. He moved to some farmland between here and that town you're from, Honeysuckle Grove. He claimed he was moving there to be closer to his family, but the rest of us owners, we knew he was about to lose his shirt."

"What was the man's name?" I hadn't made many notes during this interview, but I had my pen poised over my notepad now. "And what was the name of his store?"

"It was called The Home Store. Who knows if it's even still open, but the guy's name was James something-or-other. That's all I can tell you."

I jotted down "James" and "The Home Store."

"I offer specialty shoes, so I know I'm not really one to talk, but specialty stores, they usually don't fly in an outlet mall," he told us, as though he'd been observing as much for years. "The Home Store had all sorts of weird knickknacks. You know, like hand-carved whistles and hand-woven blankets, but not just any kind of wool. Specialty yarns like vicuna and muskox. Most items selling for hundreds of dollars." He shook his head. "Some of the store owners at the mall like me had personal grievances with Blakely, but some like James just didn't have a clue about good business. I can't imagine he ever turned a profit or could keep up on his lease payments, and the next thing I knew, he was packing up all his goods and moving on. It was right around the time I got booted from the mall, so the situation was on my radar."

I nodded and made notes of all of this.

"Please don't leave town," Amber told Barry, the same we'd heard Alex instruct suspects a dozen times. "We'll be back if we have any further questions."

As Barry retreated into his house, we turned for my car, and that was when a Juniper Mills police car decided to grace us with its presence. The two policemen inside were busy in an animated conversation with one another and didn't even register our presence at first. Apparently, Juniper Mills boasted some of the same lackadaisical police staff as Honeysuckle Grove.

"See, I told you there was nothing to worry about in interviewing this guy on our own. You're ridiculously overprotective." Amber scooped up Hunch, rolled her eyes at me, and then waved at the police car as we passed it. In her most sarcastic tone, she called out, "Thanks so much for all your help!"

Chapter Twenty-eight

BEFORE LEAVING THE NEIGHBORHOOD, we darted over to Brad's house next door. He was on a lunch break from work, but was quick to confirm Barry's alibi for New Year's Eve. He also gave us the phone numbers of three other neighbors who would be able to confirm it. Brad also told us that while Barry had held a grudge against Winston Blakely, it was more out of competitiveness to show him what he'd missed out on than wishing the old man ill will.

"What next?" Amber asked as soon as we were back in my car.

I sighed. "Do you want to Google The Home Store? If it really is between here and Honeysuckle Grove, we might as well look into it on our way back."

Amber's thumbs flew over her phone, and a handful of seconds later, she flashed me her screen, which indeed showed an address on the highway between Juniper Mills and Honeysuckle Grove.

It didn't seem likely to be connected to the case, but after how hard Amber had worked on her schoolwork yesterday to spend the day investigating, I was willing to question a few more periphery suspects to make us both feel like we were contributing.

Amber's mind continued to whir with ideas and questions as I drove. "What do you think about what Mr. Rhodes said about Jackie Reed? Do you think she was really flirting with him, or do you think she only wanted to buy nice shoes?"

"Six pairs in a row?" I raised my eyebrows.

"Yeah, I guess. I just kind of felt like that Barry guy had an overinflated ego, you know?"

She was right. Still, it didn't make him guilty of murder, even if he had overstated things between him and Winston's mistress. "Do you think it's worth questioning her again before she leaves town?"

Amber sighed and flopped back into her seat. "Probably not, but what does that leave us with? This James guy, he might have been angry with Winston Blakely six months ago, but we have no other reason to think he was connected in any way to the murder."

I had no idea why I was surprised that Amber had caught on to how ineffective this next stop probably was. She was more astute than any investigator of any age.

I was about to open my mouth to try and placate her when my phone started playing Alex's ringtone. "Grab it, would you?" I told Amber.

She quickly put him on speakerphone. "What's up? We're just on our way back from Juniper Mills. Barry Rhodes turned out to have a strong alibi for New Year's Eve."

Leave it to Amber to rattle off all of the important details in two short sentences. I likely would have gone on with all the many details of the interview before listening to what Alex had to say.

"Well, it turns out that Bob had some interesting information for me," Alex said. He sounded less tired and more energized, which made me suspect he'd been given some groundbreaking news.

"Interesting how?" Amber and I both asked at once.

"Winston Blakely definitely died of asphyxiation, but while studying particles found during the autopsy, Bob picked out several fibers that he narrowed down to be from alpaca wool."

I pulled over at the next large shoulder and looked at Amber with wide eyes. "Alpaca wool? Dylan works at an alpaca farm." I said the words that we all must have been thinking.

I could imagine Alex nodding on the other end of the line. "Bob said that all evidence leads to Winston Blakely being smothered with some sort of object made from alpaca wool."

"Should we head back to Dylan and Sheila's house and question him again?" Amber asked. Leave it to her to want to jump in once again to question the most probable suspect in a murder investigation all on our own. But, thankfully, in this case, Alex and his partner Mickey were likely much closer to Dylan's house, so I wasn't too worried.

"I already called there," Alex told us. "Sheila says he's still at the farm where he works. Mickey and I are headed there right now."

"And it's in Honeysuckle Grove?" Amber asked. I could see her hopes rising that perhaps we could get there faster than Alex.

But he said, "Yeah, on the north side," which was the opposite direction from where we were.

Amber deflated back into her seat. Hunch was on full alert, sitting on his haunches on her lap and listening to every word, but it looked as though Amber had given up.

"Okay, well, keep us updated," I told him, figuring it was up to me to do the talking at this point. "We're going to check one more place on our way back to town. Barry told us about a place called The Home Store. The owner had also been booted out of Winston's outlet mall. Apparently, they had some kind of big altercation about six months ago when he left, and they also carry some specialty wool products."

I glanced at Amber, hoping this would reignite her interest in this next stop. In truth, I was only trying to keep her busy while Alex and Mickey did their job. Too many times, we'd shown up without Alex or before him and gotten ourselves into a lot of danger with murder suspects.

If Alex was on the job, I was determined to keep the two of us—three, with Hunch—at a distance today.

Chapter Twenty-nine

AFTER WE HUNG UP, Amber was silent for most of the rest of the forty-minute drive to The Home Store. In actuality, it was much closer to Honeysuckle Grove than to Juniper Mills, and I felt bad for the owner, who likely would have had a lot more success with his store if he'd been able to secure the round building Barry Rhodes had taken over.

The building the address led us to looked like an old barn that had been—or was in the process of being—remodeled. The Home Store had a beautifully ornate hand-carved sign, but my compassion only increased when I saw there was only one truck and one car in the lot. This building may have been as big as the one Barry Rhodes had taken over for his shoe shop, but it was by far older and more weathered. It looked as though parts of it had had old boards replaced with new ones, and it was slowly being fixed up, but I was willing to bet this owner, James, didn't have the money to spruce it up the way he wanted to.

"Should we go ask the owner a few questions?" I looked at Amber, who kept her gaze out the passenger window.

"I still think we should go and help Alex with interrogating Dylan. You know, do something *useful*." She sighed. "You go ahead."

I debated what to do for a few seconds. More often than not, she was smarter than me when it came to investigative work. Should we just get back on the road and get to the alpaca farm as soon as possible? But what good could we do if Alex and

Mickey were already there? I still thought we'd only end up being in the way.

Better, I decided, to stall until we heard back from Alex. At least Amber couldn't drive on her own yet, and this was my car, so she was pretty much at my mercy until I drove her back to town.

"Fine," I said in my most responsible voice. "Do what you like, but I'm going to continue to follow all angles until we hear back that the case is tied up."

I grabbed my purse and then reached for the door. Hunch surprised me when he hopped over to my empty seat and out the door after me.

"Oh, *you're* coming?" I said to him, but really to Amber. "I'm glad someone wants to help."

When Amber didn't react, I sighed and shut my car door, wondering how long I'd have to stall inside the store to hear back from Alex.

And when would I get used to working with a pigheaded teenager?

I wasn't sure if Hunch would be able to accompany me into the store, and I told him so on our trek toward the front entrance. At least the store was set far enough off the highway that I didn't have to worry about him being hit by a car.

Also, far enough from the highway that it likely wouldn't garner much drive-by business.

But it turned out, the glass front door held a carved wooden sign that read: CLOSED. Under that was a taped paper message: GRAND OPENING, JANUARY 28TH.

"Huh. So it's not even open yet. So much for stalling," I told my cat. I'd parked around the corner from the front entrance, so not in view of Amber, but I wasn't looking forward to going back to my car and admitting she was right, so I peered through the glass door, hoping I might find something to help me delay.

Hay bales were strewn everywhere, and at first glance, I figured maybe the place truly was just an old barn, which hadn't even begun to get remodeled into a store yet. I felt bad for the owner, as January 28th was a little more than a week away.

But upon looking closer, it seemed as though each hay bale had three or four items laid on top of it. Some were small wooden carved items; others were folded woven fabric. I couldn't tell from my vantage point what many of them were, and at first, I thought perhaps they were just someone's junk left lying around until I saw what looked like a red price tag hanging from a folded woven item.

Oh. Were these the homemade items The Home Store had for sale? The décor wasn't terribly appealing. I felt bad for the owner yet again, as he didn't seem to have much of a flair for interior decorating. I wondered if this, in part, could have been why his store hadn't done well in the outlet mall.

I was about to turn and leave when a gorgeous red-and-gray sweater caught my attention. It had been laid flat, taking up an entire hay bale. I pulled myself as close as I could against the glass, even pressing my nose right up against it, but I couldn't make out the numbers on the red tag from here.

Out of pure instinct, I reached for the door handle and pulled at it. The place hadn't even opened for business, so I expected resistance. It surprised me when the door freely swung open in my hand.

I stood stunned in place, not sure what to do. I'd given Amber too many warnings to count about breaking and entering, but then a second later, my cat sauntered through the door as though he owned the place.

"Hunch, no!" I hissed. "We can't go in there!"

But of course, Hunch didn't listen. In fact, he strode straight for the middle of the shop, sat on his haunches, and looked around as though he had all day to do so. Hunch and Amber made some kind of a pair.

Then again, maybe I *was* ridiculously overprotective and should stop being such a wimp.

I tiptoed inside with the intention of grabbing my intrusive, disobedient cat and getting back out as quickly as possible, but he stood back up and moved to the rear of the store.

I'd barely gotten to the beautiful sweater when I saw the tall wooden structure Hunch was headed toward. Was that...? It couldn't be.

The missing grandfather clock?

Hunch was sniffing around the base of the clock by the time I made it over to him. I reached down to pick him up, but he swatted at my hand and growled at me.

I pulled away. I wasn't about to get ripped to shreds over it. Besides, why was the missing grandfather clock here? Upon closer inspection, I could tell it was definitely the same one, right down to the intricately designed porcelain corners. I had stood right beside it all evening on New Year's Eve, after all.

I whipped out my phone and snapped a quick photo, then navigated to my text app and quickly sent the shot off to Alex, along with the caption: ~**Look what I found at The Home Store!**~

Barry Rhodes would be relieved we'd found it. So would Chad and Alex and even the bank for that matter. But Amber and I had discussed the possibility that the missing clock had something to do with Winston Blakely's murder, and only a second later, I decided I'd better get out of here.

Hunch had moved on to sniffing other items he could reach atop hay bales. Either the hay or the woven items were bothering his nose because he pulled back. As his nose spasmed in response, I looked for my opportunity to grab him without personal injury. But before I could, two male voices came from outside the rear of the store.

"Come on! We have to get out of here," I whisper-hissed at Hunch.

The voices got louder. If the men decided to come in through the rear entry, I wouldn't make it to the front door in time. One more glance at the grandfather clock, and I made a split-second decision to hide. Maybe I'd hear something incriminating before Alex had a chance to get here.

Hunch, I decided as I dove behind a stack of hay bales in the corner, would have to fend for himself.

If it was me and I found a cat inside a store that looked like a barn, I'd pick him up and throw him out the door, and that would be the end of it. Or, if he had his claws out, I'd grab one of the nearby rakes or shovels along the wall and chase him out. Hunch wasn't cat-like in many ways, but I was pretty sure he'd take the hint and run out of here if being chased with a shovel.

A creak sounded, and the rear door opened. The voices immediately got louder.

"All I'm saying is that my boss isn't going to front you any more stock until you pay for the lot I already delivered." The voice was familiar, but before I could place it, something rubbed against my leg, nearly making me scream.

I quelled my sounds, holding a hand over my mouth when I saw it was only Hunch. It made sense. If Hunch had a choice of being booted out of the store or hiding away to listen and sniff out any more clues, it was pretty obvious which he would choose.

"How am I going to pay for this first lot when the store isn't even open yet?" an older, gruffer voice said. "It's supposed to be a *grand* opening. That means having lots of grand—"

His words were cut off by another, younger, voice. "Wait, what the heck, Dad? You have the clock on display *here*?"

In that second, I recognized the younger one's voice. It was Dylan, Sheila's live-in boyfriend and fiancé.

"Of course, I'm displaying the clock. It's only a week until my grand opening, a week until your wedding!"

"But the police are still looking for it. I had some special consultants at my house the other day asking questions. You need to hide it away, at least until things cool off."

"I don't *need* to do anything, Dylan. Your baby is on the way, and now I'm the *only* grandfather." He chuckled. "Blakely thought he could cut our whole family out of being associated with my grandchild? Sic his lawyers on me, and next thing we knew, I bet he'd have taken away *your* parental rights as well. But I've solved it now. You'd better believe I plan to display this clock proudly every chance I get."

I sucked in a breath. The clock had a meaning of Only. This James, who had fought with Winston and gotten kicked out of his mall, was the same man who was about to be a father-in-law and a grandfather. Winston had wanted James to have nothing to do with the grandchild. No wonder Sheila and Dylan were planning a shotgun wedding.

It all made sense. James had killed Winston to keep his claim to his son's first child.

What didn't make sense was Dylan's wary reaction to his dad's statement. "What do you mean, you solved it? Tell me you didn't do anything to Winston Blakely."

"The less you know, the better, son."

A long silence passed. Eventually, Dylan went on, slowly working his way to his own hypothesis. "You haven't been the same since Mom died. You're not always thinking clearly." His voice turned emotional. Almost frantic. "But things were going so well—"

"Going well? *Well?* No, things were not going *well.*"

The air in their conversation was building to a confrontation, but what could I do about it? I was hiding behind a hay bale, armed with nothing but an ornery cat.

"What did you do?" Dylan sounded near tears.

"Just calm dow—" James started.

But as if the universe heard my inner question, right at that second, Hunch let out a loud sneeze, and James cut off his sentence mid-word.

Chapter Thirty

IN AN INSTANT, I made a decision and threw my cat metaphorically under the bus and literally toward the end of the hay bale I was hidden behind, hoping it might look as though he'd jumped there.

"What's this?" Dylan asked, his voice perking up and coming closer.

Thankfully, Hunch caught on to my plan and moved between the bales and out into the open, effectively taking Dylan's attention from my hiding spot.

"I've had rats in here almost every day," James grumbled, as though finding Hunch was no different.

Dylan snickered. "This is exactly what you need if you've got rats. A good farm cat will get rid of them."

A good farm cat might, but Hunch wouldn't have the time of day for a rodent with no investigative sense.

"Here, kitty, kitty." Dylan sounded like he was squatting down. If I knew Hunch, he'd growl and hiss and be out the door the second one opened.

But apparently, I didn't know Hunch because next thing I knew, Dylan said, "Aw, look, Dad. He's purring."

I furrowed my brow in confusion and moved my angle slightly so I could see through a half-inch gap between two bales of hay. Dylan stood with Hunch snuggled up in his arms, lapping up his attention.

Once I saw it happening, it started to make sense. Hunch was smarter than the average cat. He knew there was still plenty to learn here, and he wasn't about to get thrown outside, away from the intel, if he had anything to say about it.

But James said, "Get that thing out of here. I already bought some traps to solve the rat problem."

"Aw, come on. I can't let him out here, right on the highway. Five minutes and he'll be hit by a car."

James let out a humorless chuckle. "You think Sheila's going to let you have a cat? And right before her wedding? Good luck with that."

His words were interrupted by a couple knocks sounding on glass. The glass door opened, and Amber's voice sounded from the entry. "Oh, hey. There you are! Sorry, my aunt and I just pulled over for a minute, and when I opened my car door, my cat shot out of there like a dart." Her voice came farther into the barn/store as she spoke, and a second later, she was within my vision. Amber was a pretty good actress, but I knew her well enough to see when her eyes settled on the grandfather clock, and in about a second, her computer-like brain put together everything it had taken me the last ten minutes to process.

"I see you're not open for business. So no customers yet?" Her voice held a little more strain as she looked around, probably for me. Before they had time to answer, she asked another question. "Do you have a bathroom I can use?"

"I'm afraid it's still under construction," James started to say.

Dylan interrupted him. "Hey, I know you. You came to my house with that lady from the police."

"What?" James snapped. He moved closer to his son so I got glimpses of him as well. I immediately recognized him as the man with the sideburns who had been with James at the community center on New Year's Eve and at Dylan's townhouse the first time I'd been there. But now his face was red and angry as recognition struck for him as well. "What is she doing here?" He hissed the words as though Amber wouldn't be able to hear them, only two feet away.

"I'm not sure what you're talking about." Amber's voice trembled, but I could sense her using all of her energy to steady it. "I only came to find my cat. If you'll just..." She reached out toward Hunch, but Dylan wasn't letting go. She took two quick steps back, moving out of my vision. "I'll just be on my way, then."

"Oh, no, you won't!" James said. He rushed through my vision, and a second later, Amber let out a loud gasp.

Chapter Thirty-one

AMBER LET OUT GROANS and grunts of effort, but I couldn't see her from here.

"I took care of that old man, and I'll take care of this little troublemaking girl, too." James's voice sounded strained, as though it was taking some effort to contain Amber.

I held my breath, and every muscle in my body tensed. What did he plan to do to her?

James answered my question before I had fully thought it. "Bring me that blanket, Dylan. Alpaca wool is definitely good for something. I'll smother her the same way I smothered that old man, and nobody will be the wiser."

My eyes widened, and I scrambled to the end of my hay bale to try to see what was happening.

"What? No, Dad. You can't do this! She's a good kid."

"I have to do this, Dylan. Don't you get it? She's with the police."

"I'm not!" Amber sputtered. "It was my aunt, but I won't tell her any—"

Just as they came into view, James clapped a hand over her mouth. She looked terrified and tired, like he'd already wrestled all the fight out of her. My eyes darted around in every direction for something that would help me free Amber. I wasn't about to let James smother her, and I would do everything in my power to stop it.

There was a rake across the barn, leaning against a wall, but I wouldn't get there without one of the men grabbing me first.

A shovel was closer. Still likely too far, but James had his hands full, and maybe Dylan would hesitate.

"One of these days, you're going to have to grow up and deal with your own messes." James wrenched Amber tightly in his arms, and she let out a squeak of protest.

That was my cue.

I used both of my shaking hands to spring up and toward the wall of the barn. My foot slipped on some hay, but I caught myself before completely falling and tried to get some momentum toward the shovel.

"That's her!" Dylan said.

At the same time, his dad said, "Grab her! Now!" His voice boomed, and it must have launched Dylan into action. My hand was inches from the shovel when I was yanked back by my other arm.

Before I could blink, Dylan had both my wrists tight in his hands, and he looked back at his dad for direction. While his attention was diverted, I kicked at his legs and yanked my arms down and away, but I felt as though I was making about as much difference as a tiny insect might. He jerked me tighter to him. I wondered if alpacas ever had to be wrestled into submission. Whatever the case, Dylan's farming background was clearly enough to subdue my fight unless I had some kind of a weapon.

James snapped a blanket from the hay bale I had been hiding behind. "This must be the *aunt* you were talking about?" His voice was calmer than I expected. "Because if we have two police spies, it's time for you to man up. I'm going to need your help."

Dylan's hands were rough and callused, and he was clearly strong enough to do anything his dad asked, but I'd seen a soft side of him that was our only hope.

"We've just been looking for that clock," I murmured, hoping only Dylan could hear me and James wouldn't. "If you just give it back, even anonymously, this can all go away. No one has to get hurt here."

James scoffed, clearly hearing my words. "We'll do what we have to in order to shut the two of you up. Permanently," he added. "And I'm keeping my clock. By next week, the Blakely name will be as dead as the two of you."

"Dad, I can't—"

James scoffed again. "I know *you* can't. Don't you worry. I'll take care of you once again as long as you do what I say. You know what'll happen if you don't." He offered a piercing glance in his son's direction, and in that second, I had no doubt there had been a long history of abuse in this family. "Just hold her until I'm done with this one."

James was much stronger than Amber and now had both her arms secured in one of his meaty hands. She tried to fight against him again, but he pulled her back against his chest, hard. She started to scream, but his other hand smashed an orange-and-brown, tight-woven blanket against her face, muffling her cries.

I yanked at my own arms with renewed vigor. Dylan had one in each of his hands, practically pulling my shoulders out of their sockets to subdue me, and so I used my feet again to kick at him. "You can't do this to her! You're not a killer, Dylan! Don't do this!"

"I'm sorry, Mallory. I'm so sorry," he murmured, closing his eyes as if he could block out this whole situation. But even though my words might have been hitting him, Dylan was so much stronger, and he wasn't letting up the pressure. I feared Amber would be too short on oxygen before I could sway him from his dad's agenda.

"Think of your new wife! Your new baby!" I said.

James called, "Shut her up, Dylan, or you'll be next!" and his voice boomed with authority.

I continued to wrestle against Dylan, but his dad's authoritative voice had knocked him into submission. He pushed me back against a wall, held both my wrists up against my chest with one of his hands, and cupped the other over my mouth. I desperately fought, but I was quickly losing my stamina.

There was only one thing to do. I'd been in death-defying situations before and never had much hope of surviving my horrible circumstances. But Amber had told me more than once that I was growing in my faith. I hadn't believed her before, but maybe it was true.

Because I knew my only hope was to pray.

Not only that, but I knew God would somehow come through to save us.

Chapter Thirty-two

GOD, IT TURNED OUT, sometimes worked through felines.

Only a second later, Hunch, who had disappeared after Dylan dropped him, reappeared at James's feet. He jumped and dug a claw into a corner of the blanket that hung down near his thighs and then, in a flash, climbed his way up to dig his sharp claws into James's face.

James let out something that could only be described as a shriek as he released Amber, slapped Hunch away, and reached for his claw-marked face. Even past his hands, I could see there was a lot of blood.

The move had a secondary effect of distracting Dylan. As his grip on me loosened, I whirled around and brought my knee up between his legs, then I pushed him away. Hard. By the time he righted himself, I had the shovel wielded in my hands, ready to strike him with it, and Amber had the front glass door open, where I could see Alex's unmarked police car skidding to a stop.

Seconds later, Alex and Mickey raced through the door with their guns drawn. Thankfully, both James and Dylan knew when they'd been beaten and held their hands up in the air. One clear look at James and I could tell Hunch had done a good job of intervening. Long scratch marks marred both sides of his face, and it even looked as though Hunch had gotten a claw into one of his bloodshot eyes.

We were all going to be okay, once again thanks to Hunch.

It didn't matter how tired I was. I'd have to bake up a tuna surprise for that courageous cat for dinner.

Chapter Thirty-three

"I CAN'T BELIEVE WE'RE still catering their wedding," Amber said from beside me at my kitchen counter a couple of weeks later. "I can't believe you said you would."

It did seem pretty unimaginable that we were still slated to cater a wedding for a groom who had meant to help his dad kill us only a couple of short weeks ago. As it turned out, Sheila went into labor the day their wedding had originally planned to be held, so it had been postponed, which had given me time to gain a little perspective.

I sighed and rolled out a slab of dough onto my floured countertop to prep for some cranberry sweet rolls. "Yeah, well, when it came down to it, I don't think Dylan could actually hurt anybody."

"Right. He would have only stood by while his dad committed his second murder. And his third." Amber rolled her eyes at Alex, who only smirked in her direction. "I'm just glad Detective Martinez will be there to protect us at the church."

Alex wasn't on the official invite list to the small ceremony, but that was my condition if Sheila still wanted us to cater. Dylan was still suffering the realization of all his dad had been capable of.

The second Alex had walked through the glass door into The Home Store two weeks ago, James threw up his hands and declared, "This was all my fault. My son had nothing to do with it." It didn't make up for what he had done to Winston

Blakely or what he planned to do to us, but I was glad he had said it for Dylan's sake.

In truth, Amber and I could have testified against Dylan as an accessory to attempted murder, but after much deliberation with Alex, we decided that, with his dad in prison, Dylan wasn't a danger to anybody. He would be looking at some community service hours for conspiring to steal an expensive antique clock—his dad had run the cube van driver off the road, but Dylan had helped move the clock to his dad's truck on New Year's Eve—but Dylan's record remained clean regarding Winston Blakely's murder.

His dad, on the other hand, would be locked away for a long, long time.

I tended to agree with the former owner of the grandfather clock that perhaps it was cursed. While Barry Rhodes was thankful it had been recovered, I'd heard he'd already been in touch with Chad about finding another buyer for it.

"How many of those are you going to get out of that?" Amber raised an eyebrow at the dough I'd rolled into a twelve-by-sixteen rectangle.

I knew what she was getting at. "Look, Sheila told us to expect fifty guests at her dad's funeral, and look at all the prep work that went to waste. For tomorrow, she said twenty, so I'll prepare twenty of everything. No going over and above for her again."

Amber sighed. "You're hilarious, you know. You can forgive a guy for helping his dad try to kill us, but you can't forgive his fiancé for ordering too much food?"

When she put it like that, I did seem a little off my rocker. One of my many idiosyncrasies, I supposed.

"I'm going to leave you ladies to it." Alex stood, and Hunch followed him toward the door. Whenever Alex came by these days, Hunch usually didn't want to leave him alone. He sniffed at his legs and even purred up against him, as if begging for new case details. He wasn't as cuddly as he was with Amber, but my cat's recent attention to everyone but me was bristling my jealous side again. "I have to get back to the station."

Alex had dropped by to give us an update on the case details and pick up a meatball sub I'd prepared for him to reheat at the station. More often than not, he was working until well after midnight and likely not remembering to feed himself, so I helped whenever I could.

He picked up his to-go container from the table and headed for the door. "I'll pick you ladies up at noon tomorrow?"

I followed him toward the door with my flour-covered hands held up in front of me, but Amber stayed and kept slicing pinwheels on my cutting board. "Better make it eleven thirty. We want to have everything set and coffee made before the ceremony starts at one."

Alex nodded. "Okay. I'll do my best."

If I knew Alex, he'd dress in his best suit first thing tomorrow morning and then work right up until eleven fifteen at the station before coming to get us. Part of me was tempted to tell him he really didn't need to accompany us. It wasn't as though I actually thought Dylan was any kind of a threat to me or Amber.

But the other part of me suspected Alex needed a break from the heavy caseload Steve Reinhart had him working on, and at least his presence at the wedding could be projected as work.

So I held my tongue from letting him out of the commitment, waved at him as he drove away, and then headed back to the kitchen.

"You know, three catering events since New Year's must mean we're doing something right." Amber held out the platter of prepared pinwheels, spaced perfectly to look elegant, and then proceeded to tuck plastic wrap tightly around it to keep the air out overnight. "This is exciting. Our catering business is going to be booming in no time. I can feel it."

I shook my head and chuckled.

She took my head shake as a deterrent. "What? You don't want to keep catering with me?"

"I'm not saying I don't want to start a booming catering business with you, Amber." I leaned back against the counter and hoped my smirk would relax her. "I'm just saying I'm okay if our lives get a little *less* exciting for a while."

She rolled her eyes, and I poked a floured finger at her nose.

Then we got back to work. We had twenty people to serve a late lunch to the next day, and Amber was probably right. I should let go of my past food-related grievances and prep enough food to make our business look its best for tomorrow.

Now the only question was, who would be the star of the day tomorrow: the bride or my chocolate-coated raspberry cheesecake truffles?

Only time would tell.

THE END

Up Next: Murder in the Secret Cold Case

IF YOU WOULD LIKE to read on in the Mallory Beck Cozy Culinary Capers, check out Murder in the Secret Cold Case: A Mallory Beck Cozy Culinary Caper (Book 7)

Spring has arrived in Honeysuckle Grove, and now that crime has finally settled down, Mallory is excited to put her extra time into her new catering business. Despite the lack of crime, Alex has been noticeably MIA in Mallory's life, working in the background on a secretive high-profile case. Lately it's taking up every bit of his time, and it's hard for Mallory not to feel both jilted and curious.

Not meaning to—or at the very least, not completely meaning to—Mallory gets a glimpse of detailed clues on Alex's case. The information leaves her breathless, as it quickly becomes clear why Alex has kept this case a secret.

Mallory knows she shouldn't meddle, but at the same time, she can't stay out of this investigation, most importantly because she may have key information that will help solve it.

Order your copy of Murder in the Secret Cold Case now at https://books2read.com/coldcaseebook!

Have you signed up for my newsletter yet?

IF NOT, I'D LOVE to have you! My newsletter is where I share cover reveals, excerpts, and special sales. I also like to write a bonus epilogue or novella to go with each book—exclusive reading, only available to my subscribers.

Sign up now at so you don't miss a single one!

Turn the page for a couple of recipes from Mallory's recipe box...

From Mallory's Recipe Box – Cranberry Sweet Rolls

I LOVE THESE SWEET rolls because they're easy to make a day ahead of time. Simply assemble the rolls into a baking pan and refrigerate overnight. The next day, let them warm up to room temperature and then add 10 minutes to your baking time. Sweet rolls are sweet treats that won't take all day!

INGREDIENTS:

<u>Dough</u>

1 cup milk (warmed)

1 packet of yeast

3 tablespoons sugar

3 eggs

½ cup butter (melted)

1 teaspoon salt

1 tablespoon orange peel (finely grated)

5 ½ cups all-purpose flour

<u>Filling</u>

2 cups fresh or thawed cranberries

1 tablespoon orange peel (zest)

½ cup sugar

1 teaspoon cinnamon

<u>Glaze</u>

1 cup powdered sugar

2 tablespoons orange juice

INSTRUCTIONS

<u>Dough</u>

1.

In a large mixing bowl add milk, yeast and sugar. Let sit 5-10 minutes until yeast is bubbly.

2. Add eggs, butter, salt, orange zest and 2 cups of flour. With mixer running, continue adding flour 1 cup at a time. You might not need all the flour.

3. Knead for 10 minutes.

4. Place in a well-greased bowl and cover. Let stand until doubled, 60-90 minutes. Punch down and place on a flat surface.

Filling
1. Puree cranberries in a food processor. Mix in sugar, orange zest and cinnamon.

Glaze
1. Mix powdered sugar and orange juice until smooth. Set aside.

Assemble the rolls
1. Roll out dough to a 18 inch by 12 inch rectangle.

2. Add cranberry filling over the surface of the dough. Leave a small border around all edges.

3. Roll dough along long side. Pinch edge of dough together to form a seam.

4. Slice dough into 1 inch slices. Place each slice into a greased baking dish. Cover dish with plastic wrap and allow rolls to rise for 30 minutes.

5. Bake in a preheated 400-degree oven for 20-25 minutes.

6. Allow sweet rolls to cool in pan for about 10 minutes.

7. Pour glaze over rolls.

8. Enjoy!

From Mallory's Recipe Box – Layered Greek Moussaka

1. Roll out dough to a 18 inch by 12 inch rectangle.

2. Add cranberry filling over the surface of the dough. Leave a small border around all edges.

3. Roll dough along long side. Pinch edge of dough together to form a seam.

4. Slice dough into 1 inch slices. Place each slice into a greased baking dish. Cover dish with plastic wrap and allow rolls to rise for 30 minutes.

5. Bake in a preheated 400-degree oven for 20-25 minutes.

6. Allow sweet rolls to cool in pan for about 10 minutes.

7. Pour glaze over rolls.

8. Enjoy!

THIS IS ONE OF my favorite hearty recipes for a cold winter day. I call it a "Greek Lasagna" because of all the yummy layers and, of course, the melted cheese on top. Some like to make it without the layer of potatoes, but for me, the potatoes make it into a hearty one-dish meal that is sure to fill everyone up.

INGREDIENTS

Meat sauce

2 pounds ground lamb or beef
2 tablespoons olive oil
1 onion, chopped
4 garlic cloves, chopped
1 teaspoon allspice
1 teaspoon cinnamon
1 teaspoon black pepper
1 tablespoon dried oregano
2 tablespoons tomato paste
1/2 cup red wine
Zest of 1 lemon
2 tablespoons lemon juice, or more to taste
Salt to taste
Béchamel sauce
1 stick unsalted butter
1/2 cup flour
1 teaspoon salt
4 cups whole milk
4 egg yolks
1/2 teaspoon ground nutmeg
To assemble
3 large globe eggplants
1/2 cup salt
8 cups water
2-3 Yukon gold or other yellow potatoes
1 cup grated kefalotyri, mizithra, pecorino or Parmesan cheese
Olive oil
INSTRUCTIONS:
Prepare the meat sauce:

1. Heat the olive oil in a large sauté pan over medium-high heat and brown the ground meat.

2. Add the onions about halfway into the browning process. Sprinkle salt over the meat and onions.

3. Add the spices and tomato paste.

4. Once the meat is browned and the onions have softened, add the garlic, allspice, cinnamon, black pepper,
   oregano and tomato paste. Mix well and cook for 2-3
   minutes.

5. Add the red wine and mix well. Bring the sauce to
   a simmer, reduce the heat, and continue to simmer
   gently, uncovered, for 20 minutes. Turn off the heat.
   Season with salt to taste.

6. Add the lemon zest and the lemon juice. Mix well and
   taste. If the sauce needs more acidity, add more lemon
   juice.

7. Set the sauce aside.

Prepare the potatoes and eggplants:

1. Mix the 1/2 cup salt with the 8 cups of water in a large
   pot or container to make a brine for the eggplants.

2. Slice the top and bottom off the eggplants. Peel thick
   strips of the skin off the eggplants to give them a
   striped appearance. (A little skin on the eggplant is
   good for texture, but leaving it all on makes the moussaka hard to cut later, and can add bitterness.)

3. Slice the eggplant into 1/4 inch rounds and drop them
   into the brine. Let the eggplants sit in the brine 15-20
   minutes, then remove them to a series of paper towels
   to dry.

4. As the eggplants are brining, peel and slice the potatoes into 1/4 inch rounds. Boil them in salted water for
   5-8 minutes – you want them undercooked, but no
   longer crunchy. Drain and set aside.

5. To grill the eggplant rounds, get a grill very hot and close the lid. Paint the eggplant rounds with olive oil and grill 2-3 minutes per side. Or to broil, line a broiling pan or roasting pan with aluminum foil. Paint with olive oil. Place the eggplant rounds on the foil. Broil for 3-4 minutes until lightly browned on each side. Set aside.

Prepare the béchamel:

1. Heat the milk in a medium saucepan on medium heat until steamy. Do not let simmer.

2. Melt the butter in a large saucepan over medium heat. Slowly whisk in the flour. Let this roux simmer over medium-low heat for a few minutes. Do not let it get too dark.

3. Little by little, pour the steamy milk into the roux, stirring constantly. It will set up and thicken dramatically at first, but keep adding milk and stirring and the sauce will loosen. Add the nutmeg and a teaspoon of salt. Stir well.

4. Whisk the egg yolks in a bowl. Temper the eggs so they don't scramble when you put them into the sauce: Using two hands, one with a whisk, the other with a ladle, slowly pour a couple ladles of hot béchamel into the eggs, whisking all the time.

5. Once it's warmed up, slowly pour the egg mixture back into the béchamel while whisking. Keep the sauce on very low heat. Do not let simmer or boil.

Finish the moussaka:

1. Preheat the oven to 350°F. Layer a casserole with the potatoes, overlapping slightly. Top the layer of potatoes with a layer of eggplant slices (use half the slices).

2. Cover the layer of potatoes and eggplant with the meat sauce. Add the remaining eggplant slices on top of the meat sauce.

3. Sprinkle half the cheese on top. Ladle the béchamel over everything in an even layer. Sprinkle the rest of the cheese on top.

4. Bake at 350°F for 30-45 minutes, or until the top is nicely browned.

5. Let rest for 10 minutes and then serve and enjoy!

Notes:

For a low-allergen béchamel sauce, try the following ingredients:

4 tablespoons dairy-free buttery spread
4 tablespoons sweet white rice flour
1 cup unsweetened dairy-free half-and-half
1 cup water, plus additional as needed
½ teaspoon salt, or to taste
½ teaspoon nutmeg

Acknowledgements

THANK YOU TO MY amazing team of advance readers, brainstormers, and supporters. It's getting to be such a long (and wonderful) group of people, but I am so very thankful for every single one. And to you, Reader: I appreciate you just for picking up this book and giving it a chance!

Thank you to my developmental editor, Louise Bates, my copyeditor, Sara Burgess, my "Strange Facts Expert" Danielle Lucas, my cover designer, Steven Novak, and illustrator, Ethan Heyde.

Special thanks to the book bloggers and bookstagrammers who have shared about my books, and for anyone who has taken the time to share them with their own social media following.

Thank you for joining me, along with Mallory, Amber, Alex, and Hunch on this journey. We're thrilled to have you along on this ride!

THE TABITHA CHASE DAYS of the Week Mysteries

Book 1 - Witchy Wednesday

Book 2 - Thrilling Thursday

Book 3 – Frightful Friday

Book 4 – Slippery Saturday

Mystery Anthology (Including Book 5 – Dead-end Weekend)

The Mallory Beck Cozy Culinary Capers:

Book 1 – Murder at Mile Marker 18

Book 2 – Murder at the Church Picnic

Book 3 – Murder at the Town Hall

Christmas Novella – Mystery of the Holiday Hustle

Book 4 – Murder in the Vineyard

Book 5 – Murder at the Montrose Mansion

Book 6 – Murder during the Antique Auction

Book 7 – Murder in the Secret Cold Case

Book 8 – Murder in New Orleans

Find all the Mallory Beck novels at bit.ly/MalloryBeck!
Collaborative Works:

Murder on the Boardwalk
Murder on Location
Saving Heart & Home
Nonfiction for Writers:
Writing with a Heavy Heart
Story Sparks
Fast Fiction

Denise Jaden is the author of the Mallory Beck Cozy Culinary Capers and the Tabitha Chase Days of the Week Mysteries. She is also the author of several critically-acclaimed young adult novels, as well as the author of nonfiction books for writers, including the NaNoWriMo-popular guide Fast Fiction.

In her spare time, Denise acts in TV and movies and dances with a Polynesian dance troupe. She lives just outside Vancouver, British Columbia, with her husband, son, and one very spoiled cat.

Sign up on Denise's website to receive bonus content (you'll find clues in every bonus epilogue!) as well as updates on her new Cozy Mystery Series.

www.denisejaden.com

Made in the USA
Monee, IL
14 December 2023

49123119R00121